THAT WHICH IS HIDDEN

THAT WHICH IS HIDDEN

By

S. Louisiana Doby

ISBN: 1-58820-687-4

1stBooks - rev. 7/25/01

DEDICATION

I DEDICATED THIS BOOK TO MY MOTHER FRANKIE THOMAS DOBY AND MY AUNT WILLIE JO THOMAS WHO LOVED AND SUPPORTED ME DOWN THROUGH THE YEARS. I KNOW THERE WERE TIMES WHEN I WAS GOING THROUGH MY STRUGGLES THE WAY I HANDLED THEM YOU DID NOT APPROVE BUT YOU DID NOT GIVE UP ON ME. YOUR CONSTANT PRAYERS, SUPPORT, AND COMMITMENT TO MY GOALS ALONG WITH MY COMMITMENT AND FAITH IN OUR FATHER GOT ME THROUGH SOME DIFFICULT TIMES IN MY LIFE. I LOVE YOU BOTH DEARLY

ACKNOWLEDGMENTS

To my Pastors, friends, and family you played a significant part in my accomplishing this goal. To Pastor Robinson who has been like a Father to me. Thank you for your prayers, your time, your advice, your teaching, and your support. To Pastor Thompson I appreciate the time you took out of your busy day to counsel me during some difficult times in my life. To Pastor Adams thank your for your prayers and your advice to hang in my struggles and let our Father work it out. To Minister Brunson thank you for giving me a job when I was out of work, for your prayers every time I began to talk crazy, and your help with the title of my book without you knowing it. To Lajuana & Tim Rogers for opening up your home to me when I had to start over. To Katrina & Kerry Sneed for your prayers and support as I look for work. To Linda Fripp for your prayers and support in spite of some difficult times you were going through. To Betty & Larry King who always made sure I had food to eat and gas in my car to look for a job. To Joy and Gwen thank your for your love and support. To my editor Sandra Daniels thank you for taking time out to edit my book. I thank my publisher 1st Books for taking a chance on little ole me in making one of my dreams become a reality.

Chapter One

Are You Disguising

And Saul disguised himself, and put on other raiment, and he went, and the two men with him, and they came to the woman by night: and he said, "I pray thee, divine unto me by the familiar spirit, and bring me him up, whom I shall name unto thee. I Samuel 28:8, KJV

Why do so many of us who profess to be Christians and Saved put on so many disguises? Our Father created each of us unique and special. He gave each and every one of us our very own personalities to carry out our specific purposes while here on earth. We will never become what our Father has called us out to be as long as we are disguising. We will never become shaped into what our Father created us to be as long as we are disguising. We will not know what our purposes are in this life until we become genuine in the things we do while here on earth.

Saul was a person chosen by the people of God to be their king. God allowed Saul to be king for a time until Saul outright disobeyed God. As a result of Saul's disobedience he was rejected by God as king over Israel. Saul then became desperate and allowed the spirit of disguise, the spirit of deception, and the spirit of lying to take root in his heart. Saul knew this was wrong, but he did what he wanted to do just as so many of us who are professing to be Christians and Saved, in our day and time.

The spirit of disguise can take on many different forms. This spirit can cause individuals to change appearance and lie to try and get something that was meant for someone else as Saul did. (See I Samuel 28:20, KJV). This spirit can cause individuals to pretend they were called by God to be priests, prophets, pastors, and teachers for all the wrong reasons. This spirit can cause individuals to pretend they are our friends and at the same time stab us in the back. This spirit can cause individuals to pretend they are husbands while all the time wanting other men. Some of these individuals are teaching false doctrine, some teach no doctrine, some lie that God told them to do or say something to his people, some lie that God told them to get money from His people so they can live the Life of Riley, and some leading people away from God by their leadership. We definitely have these types of individuals in our day and time just as it was back in the days of old. (See Jeremiah 23, KJV). These individuals come pretending to be of God, knowing deep down they don't even know God. These individuals are outlaws in the kingdom and some of them are not a part of the kingdom of God. They are just standing before God's people perpetrating because they understand most of us judge by what we see. (See John 8:42-43, KJV). This is the reason we have so many of us professing to be Christians and Saved, hearing the word of God but doing whatever makes us feel good for the moment, going by what we think as opposed to what has been left here for us, His word.

The spirit of disguise causes individuals to appear natural but deep within are unnatural. These individuals sit in deception trying to convince themselves and others that God created them unnatural. These individuals know deep within themselves they became what they were by living their lives independent of God. They became what they were because of what they grew up around. They became what they were because of the spirit they were born with that was not of God. (See Romans 1:21-32, KJV).

The spirit of disguise causes individuals to perpetrate, to get a person that was meant for someone else, as King David did. (See Samuel 11:3-4, KJV). We are faced with the spirit of disguise in some form every single day of our lives while here on earth. There are individuals pretending to be single but married to someone else. Some pretending to be working and at the same time selling drugs or mooching off someone else. Some wanting to date individuals for years without committing to them, just wasting their time. Some pretending they can do so much and doing nothing but talk with no action behind what they say. Some walking off from their responsibilities. We give to these individuals what belongs to the person God really has for us and this causes us to struggle. We give our time that could be spent in a relationship with our Father, becoming what He desires us to become, in order that we may be prepared for the one He has prepared for us. We give our bodies to these individuals to tear down and misuse. We put our energy into these individuals that could be used towards seeking what our purposes are in this life while here on earth. The spirit of disguise can take root in our hearts and will become whatever we want it to become to us for a time, when we are not comfortable with who we are in Christ Jesus.

In the beginning of our relationships, some of us just say things we think the other person wants to hear. We do things we think the other person likes. If this way of thinking is really a reflection of who we are, our personality, and our actions are sincere in what we are doing, it is all good. If this way of thinking is only to lure a person into a relationship with us or to get something, we are allowing the spirit of disguise, the spirit of deception, and the spirit of lying to take root in our hearts just as Saul did.

The person we disguised ourselves to get came into the relationship with us based on the personality that was shown prior to them actually becoming involved with us. The individuals disguising, know they perpetrated themselves but the person they are trying to impress may not know this at the time. Once we enter into the relationship and we see changes in these individuals, we tend to make excuses for their behavior. But actually our Father is manifesting that which was hidden about that individual's personality. These individuals are being uncovered. Instead of us putting our track shoes on and running, we make excuses for the ways we are being mistreated. We find ourselves blaming others as opposed to seeing these individuals for what they are. We blame their behavior on ex-girlfriends or ex-boyfriend, ex-husbands or ex-wives, their friends, their families, their jobs, or whatever these individuals have said are the cause for the changes. As we sit back and accept being mistreated we send out mixed signals to these individuals. They know they are wrong and we know in the relationship they are wrong. Going along with individuals when they are wrong is as if we are saying it is okay for you to disrespect me. When we know better we should expect to be given the same respect that we give regardless of an individual's past experiences. So we do not have to accept these tired excuses for being mistreated unless we do not care about ourselves and the instructions our Father has left us. Some of us even stoop to harassing ex's behind what these individuals have put into their spirits. Only our Father knows the underlying motives behind the things we do, the things we say, and the reasons we make excuses to accept bad treatment from the spirit of the enemy.

Sometimes we get so wrap up in ourselves that we forget while we are trying to deceive people, our Father is looking down on us and knows our heart. We as a people fall time and time again for what we see. We seem to forget what looks good is not always good for us, neither is it always good to us. God tells us in His word that the heart is deceitfully wicked and no one can know the motive of an individual but Him. (See Jeremiah 17:9-10, KJV). This is the reason we should always consult our Father on everything we desire. We should pray for His Will to be done in our lives and wait on Him.

Saul had an underlying motive for disguising himself and trying to deceive the witch at Endor. When God would not speak to Saul he became fearful and allowed the spirits of the enemy to attack his mind to seek "familiar or divining" spirits to speak to Samuel who was a prophet of God. These evil spirits appear to have the ability to rouse the dead from their sleep. They also seem to be able to foretell the future to some extent. God allowed this individual to know Saul's deception and the person disguising was actually Saul. God also allowed these evil spirits to raise up Samuel from his ordained sleep to pronounce Saul's doom. (See I Samuel 28:12-19, KJV).

Our Father allows us to know the personalities of the individuals we come in contact with. But of course we see what we want to see, we hear what we want to hear, and most of the time we do what we want to do. When we find ourselves attractive to an individual, sometimes we do not want to know what is being manifested to us by our Father. There are times we tend to over-look what is being manifested to us by our Father, especially those of us that have been waiting a long time for someone to come into our lives. When we are not interested in an individual our eyes are wide open and we normally see what is being manifested to us about that individual's personality.

It is a crime of fraud when you have those that profess to be Christians and Saved, marrying other individuals knowing they are crooked (homosexual) and disguising themselves to be straight. These individuals are hiding behind marriage, wanting to appear normal on the surface, and pretending to do what they know is acceptable to society. But these individuals have lied about who they are and what they are. Some of these types of individuals have the nerve to actually stand before God taking vows and making promises they know they cannot keep. Shame on em. They don't think about the fact that not only do you have two spirits at war in this type of marriage, but also a third spirit that they bring to their marriage bed if they are indeed sleeping with another individual, and sometimes can take on the personalities of the spirits that we have allowed to come into our lives.

God warns those that are disguising by saying He called them to preach while lying that He told them to tell his people a message and the message did not come from God. These individuals along with other members in their families will suffer as a result of that individual lying on God, especially when truth is not being taught. (See Jeremiah 23, KJV). The spirit of disguise is so deceiving it causes individuals to believe they can lie on God and get away with it. These evil forces want individuals to believe God called them to be church pastors while single putting themselves in compromising positions. These evil forces want individuals to be believe God is calling them to witness to others about their salvation when their own home is out of order. These evil forces want individuals to believe they can use the word of God for their gain in a deceiving way. These evil forces want individuals to believe they can give Godly counsel to married couples when they themselves have never been married and they don't know if they can do what they instruct others to do. The devil is a lie. We go along with so much that is out of God's order and we justify what we are doing by saying we are not supposed to judge. It is true we are not supposed to judge. When someone comes along saying God told them to do something that does not line up with His word we are not judging by letting that individual know what they are saying goes against the word of God. We can always pray with that individual about whatever they believe God is telling them to do. These individuals could be sincerely wrong and not have a clue that they are wrong. Sometimes other individuals can make us believe we are something that we know deep inside we are not. A lot of us are too easily influenced by others. We can find ourselves trying to be what someone else think we ought to be knowing we are not prepared by our Father. If we do not have the backbone to show someone what they are saying does not line up with the word of God we stand in judgment by our Father. We are going along with someone just to get along and this could be very dangerous. We are putting our trust in other individuals that causes us to be cursed as opposed to trusting our Father who causes us to be blessed. Listening to individuals caused the Kingdom to be snatched away from Saul. Saul feared the people that he was allowed to rule over more than he respected what God had said. He obeyed these individuals rather than hearing and obeying God. (See I Samuel 15:24, KJV). We do not have the authority to put someone in a position that goes against what our Father has instructed. The end results will always be tragic because our Father is not a part of these situations.

The struggles we have in our relationships when we disguised to get someone are struggles we have brought on ourselves. We sit in deception thinking we are fooling others, but in reality the spirit of deception has us fooled. We are living a lie. The whole relationship is based on a lie and that individual might not be the one that our Father has for us. Everything that comes from our Father is based on truth and honesty. These are good spirits that comes from His Spirit of Love along with its many characteristics.

We find ourselves praying and asking God to change the individuals back into what they showed us about themselves prior to entering into a relationship with them, not realizing they were disguising. Some of us think we can change individuals when we know they are not for real. Our Father is the only one that can change a wicked and deceitful heart. We must first be able to recognize the individuals we are in a relationship with allowed the forces of satan to use them to deceive us in some way. Once we come to this realization, we can pray that our Father change that individual's heart. The individuals disguising, have to be able to admit that they are being used by the spirit of disguise, the spirit of deception, and the spirit of lying. These individuals must have a genuine desire to change in order for our Father to change their hearts. Our Father will not force anything on us. We have to be able to admit that we need changes in our lives. We must be willing to allow our Father to make the necessary changes for our lives. Our Father knows who is suited for each of us. We usually make our own choices based on what we see, what we want, how we feel, what someone else thinks, as opposed to what has been left here for us, a love letter inspired by our Father that is His word.

Most of us believe God has a plan and a purpose for us while here on earth. Some of us go most of our lives not knowing what our purpose is in life because we are walking around here on earth allowing these evil spirits to rule our lives. Once we become genuine, our true selves, and truly under subjection to the Will of our Father, only then will we know our specific purpose while here on earth.

Chapter Two

Are You Sitting In Denial

Denial is a spirit that wants to keep us all bound by our experiences of the past. Most of these experiences started with our childhood. Abuse that we saw inflicted upon our love ones. Abuse that was inflicted upon us by those we trusted and loved. Abuse that we did to others as a result of being abused. We are what we know as far as the spirit we are born with. It starts in our homes with our childhood. When abuse is not recognized, acknowledged, and dealt with, it is carried into adulthood. Individuals that carry abuse into their adult life, seem to function well in every day life, but in reality they are dysfunctional. They may appear to be happy, but deep within they are unhappy people. You may see them laughing on the outside, but inside they are crying out. These individuals are sitting in denial bound by their past because they have not come to grips with their past. These individuals are allowing the spirit of denial to control a certain part of their lives that they do not want known.

So many of us in our day and time use as an excuse our past to treat others the way we do not want to be treated. Most of us that use our past experiences to treat others bad cannot take any bad treatment. These individuals cannot see what they may or may not be doing as wrong, but they can see all the wrongs in someone else because they are sitting in denial. Some of us have been sitting in denial for so long that we begin to believe in our minds we are alright. This is how the spirit of denial makes us believe we are right when we are wrong.

Lot's daughters are a good example of sitting in denial bound by their past. God allowed them to be removed from Sodom, but Sodom was not removed from them. The daughters of Lot acted out on him what they grew up around, immorality. They allowed the spirit of denial to enter into their minds and caused them to believe there was not a man on earth for them. The spirit of denial put into their spirits that they needed to preserve their father's seed. They had sex with their father after they got him drunk on spirits and they both conceived. (See Genesis 19:31- 37, KJV).

The spirit of denial causes individuals to be deceived.

The spirit of denial causes individuals to block things out.

The spirit of denial causes individuals to refuse to believe or accept an experience.

The spirit of denial causes individuals to lie about the basic who they are.

The spirit of denial causes individuals not to see themselves.

Some individuals in denial are constantly in and out of relationships when face with struggles that reminds them of their past. This happens when they are not ready to deal with their past. Some individuals will pack up and leave a commitment when they are not ready to deal with their past. Some individuals go through life blaming others for everything that has gone wrong for them because they do not see themselves. Some individuals grow up in statue and are stuck in adolence because they have not learned from their past. The spirit of denial wants to keep us all chained to our past because it knows that we will eventually destroy ourselves or destroy other individuals. We will walk around here on earth confused, making the same mistakes over and over again.

The persons of Sodom were in denial big time about who they were. Apparently the two angels that came to destroy the cities of Sodom and Gomorrah were very good-looking angels (manifested as men). The individuals of the cities old and young came to Lot's house seeking these angels (manifested as men). They wanted to have sex with these angels. They wanted them so badly they were willing to break Lots door down to get to these angels. These individuals were so far in denial they lived unnaturally. (See Genesis 19, KJV).

In our day and time, we have those that profess to be Christians and Saved but openly crooked. (Homosexuals) These individuals are sitting in denial because they have not dealt with abuse of their past. They are holding on to what happened in their childhood by a relative, a friend, or a stranger. These individuals are using how they are living and what they are doing as an excuse to live a lie. It may have been rape, a lack of genuine love and affection, the spirits of the parents if they were homosexual, a weak father and the wrong kind of affection was shown, or maybe the the enemy put the thought in their minds and they acted upon it. We can come up with all kind of reasons as to why individuals prefer to have the same sex in a relationship as opposed to being the way God created them. Some of these individuals even lie on God and say, "God created them the way they are". (Homosexual) A lie straight from the gates of hell. The spirit of denial keeps these individuals from admitting that this is a life style they have chosen that they like for the time being. The bottom line is these individuals are sitting in denial bound by their past and comfortable with what they are doing not realizing satan has them in bondage to homosexuality.

There are those that profess to be Christians and Saved believing the biggest lie from the enemy, that God sent them a man that is already married to someone else. The spirit of denial causes both of these individuals to sit in denial. That which is hidden will be manifested and we are deceived in our minds if we think our situation is different. (See Mark 4:22, KJV). The games individuals play of this world does not change. Only the individuals playing the games change. Our Father is not the author of confusion. He will not send anybody into our lives for us to play around with that is already attached to someone else in a marriage. The enemy will do this to us to keep individuals confused. He knows not only will we sit in denial but we will also struggle.

There are those that profess to be Christians and Saved who are married, but are acting as if they are not married. These individuals are living a double life by trying to take care of someone else's home, just lost all touch with reality because they are sitting in denial. Some of these individuals are barely making it themselves and know they need every penny God has blessed them with to take care of their families. The spirit of denial attacks these individual's minds by saying to them that their families do not need everything they claim. These individuals do just enough to get by. The spirit of denial causes these individuals to lay down at night sleeping well believing in their minds they got it going on. The spirit of denial causes these individuals to feel good about paying someone else's bills. When it comes to their families they have to penny pinch, cut back, and do nothing because money that should be coming into their home is being spent in someone else's household. Shame on these individuals.

There are those that profess to be Christians and Saved who want to have sex with as many individuals as they can before they get married. Some of these individuals once they get married try to live celibate in their marriage. These individuals are sitting in denial because living celibate in a marriage cannot be done in a successful marriage. The enemy causes us to tell each other "don't touch me, and leave me alone" in our marriages. The enemy causes husbands and wives to not want to make love to each other in their marriages. The enemy causes individuals to think masturbation can take the place of making love to each other in their marriages. Love making is a gift from our Father that everybody on the face of this earth ought to love. It is something mighty wrong with an individual that wants to get married and not share the gift of love making with the person they are married to. Our Father tells us in His word how we as believers should be in our marriages. We as believers in our marriages should not deprive each other of our needs sexually. When we are depriving each other it should be an agreement between the two individuals for a time of fasting and prayer. (See I Corinthians 7:5, KJV). We are instructed by our Father to come back together again so the enemy will not tempt us because of our weaknesses in this area.

There are those that profess to be Christians and Saved who believe they have the right to marry the same sex, and at the same time believe they have the right to bring children into their messed up environment. The spirit of denial causes these individuals to believe their living environment is functional when it is dysfunctional. The spirit of denial causes these individuals to believe their living environment is normal when is it abnormal. These individuals not only sit in denial but are also selfish to bring other individuals into their messed up environment. I believe if God wanted two men to bare children together or two women to bare children together we would have been born with a penis and a vaginal together so we could choose.

There are those that profess to be Christians and Saved blaming others for everything that has gone wrong for them in their lives. These individuals are sitting in denial because they refuse to see themselves. These individuals go through life making the same mistakes, falling deeper and deeper in the same hole because they have not matured mentally.

I know this person that walked away from his wife after six months of marriage. This individual's job relocated him to another state. His wife quit her job and relocated to be with her husband. Six months into the marriage he decided he did not want to be married anymore. He took his money and all of their furniture and moved into a place of his own. He left his wife in a state where she did not know anyone and she did not have a job. This individual told others his wife caused him to leave her. When he was asked what did his wife do to cause him to leave her he replied that his wife gave him "high blood pressure, she would not let him be a man, he could not talk to her, and she was real mean." This individual ran as far away from his wife as he could blaming his wife for his actions not realizing he is responsible for his own actions. It is so sad when adults think like children. It is even sadder when adults act like children. These individuals let others around them know they are sitting in denial by their conversation and actions. When we cannot see ourselves for who we are, more than likely we are not admitting to our Father how we are. The enemy wants us all to stay blind and crippled. When we refuse to examine ourselves we cease to learn and grow.

Sitting In Denial Causes

A. **One to tote the biggest Bible and not understand anything in it.**
B. **One to think they are loving when they are hurting.**
C. **A man to become passive in his home and the roles switch.**
D. **A man to become the tail and not the head.**
E. **One to think things can be done their way and not God's way.**
F. **One to profess to know God and live their lives independent of God.**
G. **Individuals of the same sex to believe they have the right to marry.**
H. **One to blame others for their inconsistency.**
I. **Individuals to make the same mistakes over and over**
J. **Individuals to think immature because they have not dealt with their past experiences**
K. **One to become so consume with wrongs to the point of not caring about the consequences.**

It is indeed a blessing to go through struggles and come out of them in our right minds. We now have testimonies to be shared with others in similar situations as to how our Father brought us over, brought us through, and healed us. To get out of denial, we have to be able to recognize what we are allowing to control our lives; the spirit of deception, the spirit of control, and the spirit of fear. We have to be able to come to God our Father and strip naked before him by renting our hearts to Him so we can be healed of our past. Because our Father is omniscient, He already knows what we have gone through. Sharing our experiences, our mistakes, our hurts, our pains, our wrongs, and our struggles with our Father is for us to become more aware of who we are apart from Him. It keeps us from sitting in denial. It helps us to be able to learn from our experiences and recognize our mistakes. Our Father in turn heals us of our hurts and our pains. He forgives us of our wrongs when we can admit to being wrong. We can now understand our struggles are for our good and it does not matter how bad they may seem. In the process of sharing with our Father, it helps us to come to grips with the fact that we need Him in our lives daily, to help us become better individuals in spite of what we have gone through.

Psalms 139 tells us that our Father knows everything about us. There is nothing that has happened in our lives, our Father did not see and know. Our Father knows all that we have gone through. He knows what kind of homes we came from. He knows what kind of parents we had. He knows if they brought us up the way He instructed them to do. He knows what kind of spirits we had to live with in our homes. He knows everyone of us that had a father figure in our homes and those who did not have a father figure in the home. He knows those of us that were abused verbally, mentally, emotionally, and physically. Our Father saw our tears. He felt our pain. He knows the shame some of us felt. He knows about the abuse. He knows who did the abusing. He saw us abuse other individuals as a result of being abused. He already knew those of us who would sit in denial.

Sitting in denial does not mean we are fooling others just because we have been there for so long. It is our Father giving us time to come to grips with our past so we can be healed. We have to be able to talk about abuse of our past without feeling ashamed. We have to be able to admit that we have abused others as a result of being abused. We have to be able to talk about situations that are hurting us now, so the enemy will not bring up our past experiences to try and use it against us. This is how the enemy keeps us bound to our past, and keeps individuals sitting in denial by using our past experiences or past mistakes, to keep us from moving forward in this life while here on earth.

Our Father wants to heal us all of our broken hearts and demon oppressed spirits. (See Mark 1:21-45, KJV). The spirit of denial can destroy us just as our Father destroyed the cities of Sodom and Gomorrah back in the days of old. Because these people were so far in denial, they lived their lives as if there was no God just as some of us that are sitting in denial today. We cannot use in this day and time the way we live, the way we act, and the way we think, as an excuse to sit in denial when our Father has brought us over and brought us through our past experiences.

Chapter Three

Struggles We Face

For we wrestle not against flesh and blood,
but against principalities, against powers,
against the rulers of the darkness of this world,
against spiritual wickedness in high places.
Ephesians 6:12, KJV

Wake up my fellow brothers and sisters in Christ because we are in a spiritual warfare battling with the unseen. We go up against a powerful army that we cannot see every single day of our lives. The goal of this army is to defeat the Saints of God. We are faced with many different struggles in this life while here on earth. The ways we deal with our struggles have a lot to do with the evil spirit we allow ourselves to be used by while going through our struggles.

Our Father tells us in His word that our struggles are not with persons of flesh and blood. Our struggles are with persons without bodies called spirits. These disembodied spirits are wicked giants, evil rulers, unearthly beings, and satanic beings in the demonic world. Satan has control over these evil spirits. They want our bodies to occupy them so they can carry out their purpose here on earth. These evil spirits cannot perform unless they have a body to occupy and use. We as Christians allow ourselves to be used by the many forces of satan daily. When we allow them to occupy our bodies, they are not satisfied until they have tormented us or used us to torment other individuals. (See Mark 5:2-5, KJV) how these evil spirits called legions had taken over this person's body tormenting him night and day. These spirits called legions caused this person to abuse himself. This person's mind became so mixed up to the point where he made his home in a a cemetery. He began living among the dead as a mad person who had lost all touch with reality.

The goal of these evil spirits is to steal our blessings our Father has for us by causing us to live outside the Will of God. These blessings could be our families, our jobs, our money, our children, our peace, our joy, our health, or our happiness. These evil spirits want our reputations destroyed. They want our dispositions to change for the worse. They want our attitudes to become so terrible that no one will want to be around us. They want our faces to become disfigured. They want to take away our sane minds. They want us to walk around here on earth believing right is wrong and wrong is right. They want us to die spiritually. These evil spirits want to occupy our bodies to cause us to kill each other physically, emotionally, verbally, and mentally.

Some of us as Christian allow ourselves to be used by these evil spirits to the point of destruction and this is why we become defensive about the wrongs we do as opposed to what is right. Ananias, who was a Christian allowed the spirit of deception to enter into his heart and this spirit caused him to lie to the Holy Spirit. He fell dead as a result of that deception. This spirit not only deceived Ananias but also deceived his wife Sapphira and she fell dead also. These Christians individuals knew better. They thought they could get away with deceiving the people, but in reality the spirit of deception had them both fooled. (See Acts 5:2-5, KJV).

These spirits existed back in that perfect beginning in the world that was, before the foundation of this earth age, and before humanity. They are beings created by God our Father. (See Psalms 68:17, KJV). These spirits were not created evil. (See Ezekiel 28:12-15, KJV). They became corrupt in Heaven as they decided to stand-alone with satan, just as some of us that are professing to be Christians and Saved are choosing to stand with satan while we are here on earth. These disembodied spirits are the ones that are not chained under darkness in prison. They go about doing the will of satan. They watch and wait for us to slip up when we are at a weak moment in our lives. This is their opportunity to confuse our minds and occupy our bodies. This is the chance they have waited for to try and take control of our hearts to keep us from fulfilling our purpose while we are here on earth. Although they know their home is hell, this does not stop these demons from trying to get us to go to hell with them. They want us to spend eternity away from our Father because they are doomed and hell bound. Just imagine living with the same evil people that we know we cannot tolerate on earth right now that belong to satan in the next life for eternity. That is hell in itself.

Let's take a look at who we give so much credit to in this life here on earth. Satan the adversary of God and accuser of God's people, who was a deceiver from the beginning of humanity, that was booted out of Heaven, the ruler of these evil spirits, the ruler of this world system, the ruler of the air, who is cursed by God, that walks to and fro in the earth trying to snatch up as many of the Saints of God as he can. (See I Peter 5:8), (Zechariah 3:1), (John 8:44), (Isaiah 14:12-14), (Luke 10:18), (Matthew 12:24), (9:34, John 14:30), (John 12:31), (Ephesians 2:2), (Genesis 3:14), (Job 1:6, 2:1, KJV), (Revelation 9:11, KJV).

My brothers and sisters in Christ, these evil spirits are not just figments of our imaginations. Satan is not a little old red animal carrying a pitchfork with two horns and a long tail. The Word of our Father clearly teaches the reality of satan and the fallen angels. These evil spirits are also known as demons and unclean sprits. Satan and his followers are the cause of all the turmoil in this word system today. Some of these fallen angels are the principle forces behind the world powers. These evil spirits do not have a color attached to them. They can choose any of our bodies to occupy and use when we allow ourselves to be used by them.

Among these evil spirits there is rank and there rank is compared to that of the military. They have different levels of responsibility with satan being the highest-ranking evil spirit. They have order and they are in order among themselves. Their orders are carried out with force. They are persistent with trying to accomplish their goals down here on earth. These evil spirits constantly brings the same old situations to us time and time again. The many spirits of satan cause us to believe in our minds our situations are different to get us caught up in bad situations. A lot of us fall for the same old tired situations time and time again. We actually believe in our minds our situations are different. We can find ourselves in the same situations that we have talked about other individuals for getting caught up in just because the enemy presented it to us in a different way.

There are a lot of evil spirits out there in this cosmos just waiting for the right opportunity to occupy the bodies of the Saints of God. Those of us that profess to be Christians and Saved try hard to stay focused and live for Christ Jesus while here on earth, are a challenge to these evil spirits. These evil spirits do not care about those individuals that have not professed to be Christians and Saved, and those that have not given their lives to Jesus Christ. They grow weary of using these individuals because they already have them. These evil spirits know they can occupy and use the bodies of these individuals at any time because they are lost. Some of these spirits of satan have actually taken over these individual's body and will make these individuals do whatever they want them to do at any given moment.

Some of the many evil forces of satan that can occupy our bodies when we are living our lives independent of our Father are:

The Spirit of Control
The Spirit of Confusion
The Spirit of Division
The Spirit of Lust
The Spirit of Pride
The Spirit of Anger
The Spirit of Hate
The Spirit of Fear
The Spirit of Rebellion
The Spirit of Deception

These are just a few evil spirits that we allow ourselves to be used by but there are many more. These evil spirits want to turn around as many of the Saints of God as they can because they know time is running out for them.

The Spirit of Control

The spirit of control keeps us addicted to our bad habits. It may be drugs, cigarette smoking, stealing, gambling, alcohol, cheating, lying just whatever controls us to the point of compulsion. The spirit of control wants to keep us in denial bound to our habits. If the spirit of control can have just the part of us that we are hiding for whatever reason, it can keep us bound and this spirit is ruling that part of us.

The Spirit of Control occupies the bodies of those persons that are searching for some type of identity and looking to belong. This is how the spirit of control can lead families to join cults. Some of these families end up giving their lives to a false leader that is already lead by the spirit of control and this spirit will wipe out families if allowed by these people. The spirit of control occupies the bodies of those persons that are not rooted and grounded in the word of God. This spirit can cause these persons to follow after what sounds good but false doctrine. The spirit of control occupies the bodies of those persons that are insecure. This spirit causes these persons to be uncomfortable with who they are and they abuse their responsibility to feel good about themselves.

When we allow ourselves to be used by the spirit of control we lose focus. We can find ourselves caught up in many different types of bad situations. The spirit of control causes some individuals to make excuses to stay in unhealthy situations. We can find ourselves being prisoners in our homes and our needs taken away as a way of punishment just to show who is in control.

The spirit of control had a relative of mine bound to drugs. The first time he went to jail he spent seven years in prison. While he was locked up in prison he talked so good about how God protected him in prison, and showed him that he could have looked just like the other individuals in prison with him. Some of these individuals had contracted aids from doing drugs. Some of these individuals had half a body from being shot up because of drugs. Some of these individuals were dying as a result of using drugs. He talked so good about how he wanted to counsel other individuals that were hooked on drugs, when he got out of prison. When he got out of prison he was blessed with a good paying job. This job was already lined up for him when he got out of prison. That was a blessing. He worked on this job for five months before he began to resume his old life-style of selling drugs. This time he was not only selling drugs but he was also using what he was selling. He finally quit his real job and began selling drugs full time. He made life hell on earth for his family. He was out there so bad using drugs that he began selling bath soap and chipping up rocks to sell for drugs. Now yawl know he "had ran out." He was asking for death. Whenever he was not getting high on drugs, he could admit that he had a sickness and wanted help. I truly believed that he wanted to come up out of his situation but his addiction was bigger than him alone. He was allowing himself to be used by the spirit of control and it occupied his entire body. He lost weight tremendously. He began tweaking and chirping like a bird. His disposition changed for the worse. He would sleep during the day while his old lady went out to make a decent living working on a real job. He would ride around at night looking for the individuals he gave drugs to on credit and those that he sold bad drugs to. We did not give up on him. His family prayed for him constantly and also, his friends that were not using drugs. I am happy to say he has been given another chance by our Father. He is no longer on the streets selling and using drugs. He is locked away in a rehabilitation center getting the help he needs for his drug addiction. He is no longer being controlled by using and selling drugs. Prayer does changes situations.

The struggles we have when the spirit of control is occupying our bodies are abuse. We abuse ourselves by doing things to our bodies that are harmful without realizing what we are doing. We abuse our love ones because we are out of control. The spirit of control causes us to become separated from our loves ones. The spirit of control will lead us to being out of fellowship with our Father if we allow it by not recognizing the many sins we do as a result of this spirit controlling our lives.

The Spirit of Confusion

The spirit of confusion attacks our minds with an evil thought and causes us to jumble things around in our minds when we already know in our spirit what is true. The spirit of confusion is the spirit that tells us our marriage is a mistake. The spirit of confusion get into our heads and says to our minds "you put yourself together not God, this marriage was wrong from the beginning, they do not care about you, and they do not have your best interest at heart." When the spirit of confusion has planted the thought in our minds and it has taken root in our hearts, we have become turned around by this spirit. The spirit of confusion wants to rob us all of our sound minds and it will take away our minds if we allow it. The spirit of confusion causes us to become disturbed mentally and sick in the mind because it is warped. The spirit of confusion occupies the bodies of those persons that have not learned from their past experiences. This spirit wants these persons to continue to make the same mistakes over and over again.

The spirit of confusion had an acquaintance of mine out there bad living a double life. He told his high school sweetheart that God told him she was going to be his wife. She did not know any better at the time and she eventually married him. After two years of marriage he began to cheat and kept cheating with the same person. His mind became so turned around that he put his girlfriend on the same credit card with him and his wife. He would take his girlfriend out of town and would call his wife from a pay phone in the hotel where he and his girlfriend would shack-up for the weekend. He would tell his wife that he was out of town on business and he would never give his wife his room number or telephone number whenever he was with his girlfriend. His wife could never find his hotel number because he always used a different name at different hotels and he would call his wife on the pay phones in the hotel. This individual didn't know how to cheat, not that it is a certain way to cheat because eventually, all cheaters get caught. He treated his girlfriend as if she was his wife, and he treated his wife as if she was the girlfriend. He eventually lost his job and could no longer afford to take his girlfriend on weekend trips. He could no longer use his job as an excuse to take his girlfriend out of town. His wife knew he was not working but his girlfriend did not know at the time that he had lost his job. He began to write hot checks to buy food for his girlfriend and her three children trying to make her think he still had it going on. He did not care that his girlfriend and her family were eaten stolen food. He did not care that his checks were bouncing all over the state in which he lived. He suited down every day as if he was going to a job pretending to be working knowing all the time he was unemployed. He began lying to his family that his wife was taking all of his money, when in fact he did not have any because he did not have a job. He was lying to his wife that he was out getting assignments for a business he was trying to get started that never got started. He was a very intelligent man that graduated top in his class from high school and went to college on an academic scholarship. As intelligent as he was, he could not manage to keep a job or find a job during the time he was acting like an outlaw. He allowed the spirit of confusion to occupy his body to the point of destroying his marriage thinking with the wrong head. He did managed to keep his desperate girlfriend and her three children in spite of him not working. His wife eventually left him because she got sick and tired of dealing with him and his ready-made family. He married his girlfriend soon as his divorce was final.

When we allow ourselves to be used by the spirit of confusion, we walk around here on earth believing in our minds we are deep when we are mixed up. The knowledge our Father has allowed us to obtain that has been around since the beginning of time does not make us deep. The way we apply the knowledge that we are allowed to know is what gives an individual some dept. When knowledge causes us to turn away from the truth as we know it according to the word of God, you can rest assure confusion is in the midst. The spirit of confusion causes those that are mixed up in their minds to follow after the opinions of man. The spirit of confusion causes those that are mixed up in their minds to follow after what sounds good. The spirit of confusion causes those that are mixed up in their minds to question the word of God when they want to have their way. The spirit of confusion causes those that are mixed up in their mind to change their names to fit some organization or cult. Some of these individuals actually believe God is in the midst of this confusion. You better not tell these individuals they are not deep unless you are prepared for a battle with the unseen.

The struggles we have when the spirit of confusion is occupying our bodies is a lack of reasoning. We cannot reach anyone when we do not have the right understanding and the wisdom to go along with the knowledge that God has allowed us to have. The spirit of confusion causes us to be out of order and God anoints order. When we are out of order we are no longer pleasing our Father. We are pleasing ourselves for a time and walking around here on earth talking crazy, looking crazy, acting crazy, and thinking wrong. We are allowing ourselves to be used mightily by the spirit of confusion, which causes us to struggle. If we do not recognize the spirit of confusion in our lives or in the lives of our love ones, someone could end up in a mental institution being treated for a psychological problem when that person is really mixed up because of the spirit of confusion.

The Spirit of Division

The spirit of division attacks those persons that are already mixed up by the spirit of confusion and have not recognized it yet. The spirit of division comes into our lives to divide us, split us up, separate us, and to conquer us. This is the spirit that says to our minds "walk out, give up on your marriage, maybe yawl need to separate, detach yourself, become passive, you tried to make it work now go file for a divorce." The spirit of division occupies the bodies of those persons that are not committed and just looking for an excuse to be gone. The spirit of division occupies the bodies of those persons that got married for all the wrong reasons. The spirit of division knows it will not take much to drive a wedge between these individuals because someone was not sincere.

I know this individual that set out to drive a wedge between this man and his wife. She could have had just about any man that she wanted. She was beautiful on the outside, educated, with a lovable personality. She was blessed with a good paying job in her field which was Electrical Engineering. But she just had to have this one particular man that was already married to someone else. She made it real comfortable for this man by having in her home most of the things he told her he liked. She gave this individual everything he asked for including a key to her house and a key to her car. She would get high on marijuana joints and as she put it she "would ware him out."

She did not want him to have an ounce of energy to sleep with his wife. She even stooped to buying the bamboozle a car to get him. This worked for a while until he had to deal with the same problems with her that he did not want to deal with in his marriage, which was not dealing with anything. She drove a wedge between this man and his wife for a short time and lost her mind during the process. She did so much for this man that she lost herself in the midst of all that she was doing and went crazy. She allowed the spirit of division to occupy her body and she became separated from her blessings. She is now on crazy medication talking gibberish like babies talk as they begin to pronounce words. This man eventually went back to his wife and left her alone for good. He could not handle the fact that she had lost her mind. She could not handle not being with this person.

When we allow ourselves to be used by the spirit of division, we can abandoned our post and justify leaving because our minds are confused. The spirit of division causes us to live in our marriages as if we are roommates sleeping in separate rooms comfortably. The spirit of division causes us to walk around not communicating at all and our needs are not getting met.

One of the struggles we have when the spirit of division is occupying our bodies is not sharing with one another. The spirit of division causes us to walk away from our responsibility and to allow others to dictate for us what we should do in our homes. The spirit of division causes us to act as if we live by ourselves and we become indifferent towards one another. The spirit of division causes us to become passive in our homes. The spirit of division causes our roles to switch and this is how it drives a wedge between us in our homes when we allow this evil spirit to occupy our bodies.

The Spirit Of Lust

The spirit of lust makes us think we can cheat and we will not get caught in our cheating. The spirit of lust causes us to believe as long as we are not hurting anyone it is nothing wrong with cheating, but in reality we are hurting ourselves. The spirit of lust tell the same old lies to occupy our bodies. Some of us fall for the same old tired lies time and time again. The spirit of lust is the spirit that says to us "I desire only you and already committed." I just want to be with you while living with someone, me and my spouse we do not sleep together we just dwell together, therefore; we do not have a marriage and going home every night." I'm in love with you and lusting after someone else, you make me happy and at the same time this lustful spirit is married or dating someone else trying to occupy another persons body." The spirit of lust occupies the bodies of those individuals that are long eyed and greedy. The spirit of lust occupies the bodies of those individuals that is always thinking it is something better out for them in this cosmos and they are not doing jack. The spirit of lust occupies the bodies of those individuals that think the grass is greener on the other side.

When we allow ourselves to be used by the spirit of lust, we can become so intense about what we are doing that is wrong, we can justify doing it. The spirit of lust puts before us what looks good and we find ourselves desiring it. The spirit of lust puts before us what feels good and we find ourselves wanting it. The spirit of lust puts before us what taste good and we find ourselves longing for it.

I had a co-worker that had been in a relationship with a married man for five years. According to my co-worker this married man pleased her the way she wanted to be pleased sexually. This married man would come to my co-workers house whenever him and his wife got into an argument. He would talk bad about his wife, sleep with my co-worker, and go home to his wife taking her bad spirit with him. My co-worker could not understand why the wife would not leave her husband. In her mind, she felt as if the wife had to know her husband was cheating on her. She was so sure that this married man was in love with her because he did not want her to date anyone else but him, and he was giving her money. My co-worker could not see that she was allowing the spirit of lust to occupy her body and she was being used. You couldn't have told this old married man he was being used either because he acted as if he knew he had it going on. My co-worker blamed the wife for not leaving her husband as the reason why she and her married lover could not be together on a full time basis. It wasn't until this old married man lost his job and could no longer give my co-worker anymore money that he realized he was being used. He could no longer sleep with my co-woker nor would she allow him to come to her house. He found out quickly that it cost to try to be someone else's boss too. He also found out that he did not have it going on as strong as he thought he did and he was just being used. The only thing my co-worker really wanted from this old man was his old money. My co-worker finally admitted that her relationship with this man was based on lusting after what she believed he had. After this man lost his job, my co-worker ended their relationship. According to my co-worker sleeping with this old man was no longer any good. She could no longer tolerate feeling his sagging lumps and bumps because she was not getting any money. This man could not say anything to my co-worker as long as he was broke and without a job.

The spirit of lust brings with him many strong desires that causes:

- **A. Men to fornicate with men.**
- **B. Women to fornicate with women.**
- **C. Men and women to live together as if they are married and not want to commit**
- **D. Women to date married men**
- **E. Men to date married women**
- **F. Rape of all kinds**
- **G. Prostitution**
- **H. Incest**
- **I. Bestiality**
- **J. Human Beings having sex with the dead**

K. **Babies having babies**

The spirit of lust can bring into our lives many diseases such as:

A. **Aids**
B. **STD**
C. **Herpes**
D. **Gonnereah**
E. **Syphilis**
F. **VD**
G. **Vaginal Warts**
H. **Red Bugs**

This is the spirit that caused the " sons of God" of Genesis 6 to leave their habitation and come down to earth. These influctuations of the "sons of God" took wives of the "daughters of men," and bore children with them. This intrusion of certain "sons of God" into the human family resulted in an unnatural offspring called Nephilim. (Genesis 6:2-4, Companion KJV). Their sins were compared to that of Sodom and Gomarrah. (Jude 14, Companion KJV) but our Father destroyed these wicked super humans in size, abnormal beings with the flood. Because these "sons of God" allowed themselves to be used by the spirit of lust they are in prison "chained under darkness," (See II Peter 3:19&20, Companion KJV) waiting for judgment. (See II Peter 2:4, Companion KJV).

The struggles we have when the spirit of lust is occupying our bodies are the attitudes of the spirits we take upon. We do not know what kind of evil spirit we are allowing to occupy our bodies when we are thinking with the wrong head or when we want to feel good for a minute. When we bring this spirit into our homes and we inflict it upon our love ones we are killing them slowly. This spirit brings with it strongholds, and gets at some point all of us on the face of this earth. Even if the act is not carried out the spirit of lust has put lustful thoughts in our minds. Some of us can recognize this spirit and unfortunately some of us actually mistake the spirit of lust for the Spirit of Love. If we do not recognize this spirit it will destroy us to death just as our Father destroyed those individuals that mixed with the sons of God back in the days of Noah.

The Spirit of Pride

The spirit of pride causes the downfall of every person on the face of this earth. The spirit of pride occupies the bodies of those persons that want to be worshipped by mankind and those that are vain. The spirit of pride occupies the bodies of those who believe their accomplishments are based on their efforts alone. The spirit of pride wants to take us so high that when we fall we just might crack the teraferma. The spirit of pride causes us to get mighty big headed and full of ourselves. When we get to this point, we have allowed other spirits of pride to take root in our hearts. The spirit of haughty and the spirit of arrogance. Our Father tells us in His word that destruction is a result of that prideful-spirit taking root in our hearts. (See Proverbs 16:18, KJV).

I know this arrogant person who talked about his wife and her friends because they did not make as much money as he thought they should have been making. He would tell them they were working for pennies compared to his salary. He would make his wife drive an old beat up car to work that could barely make it around the next block while he leaned to the side in his Jaguar. He would insult his wife's friends by calling them fat when you could hear him crunching in his clothes as he walked because his thighs would rubbed together. This person could not be told anything because he knew everything. One evening as he was screaming insults at his wife in front of her friends, he fell to the ground. He thought he was having a heart attack but his big rump was actually having a gas attack. The same individuals he talked about were the ones who rushed him to the hospital and gave moral support to his wife. This experience changed him for the good. He admitted to his wife and her friends that he was allowing the evil spirit of pride to take over him.

When we allow ourselves to be used by the spirit of pride no one can tell us anything. We act as if we are in relationships by ourselves, we only think about what we want, and we take our blessings from our Father for granted. The spirit of pride causes some of us to become snooty and look down on others believing we are better because of our blessings from God.

The struggles we have when we allow the spirit of pride to occupy our bodies is selfishness. The spirit of pride causes us to act as if the world revolves around us. The spirit of pride causes us to be stingy and think only of ourselves. We can see this spirit on our jobs with individuals that are hung up on titles and power. They allow themselves to be used by the enemy to watch other individuals, to snitch on individuals, and will do whatever it takes to get them fired. We see the spirit of pride in our marriages. When we start telling each other out of anger, "this is my house so you get out, this is my money and I can do what I want, I bought this car and you can't drive it, I pay these bills and I don't have to answer to you, I don't need you, I don't care what you do, and I am leaving you," we are allowing ourselves to be used by the evil spirit of pride. The selfish attitude of living our lives independent of our Father and giving ourselves credit for the blessings He has given us is very dangerous. Satan had the same selfish attitude before he got kicked out of Heaven. When satan said, "I will," sin began. (See Isaiah 14:12-17, KJV). Sometimes this spirit causes us to choose our mates based on superficial reasons, such as; what we think someone has, what we believe they can do for us, what kind of car the individual drives, if they have a college degree, what kind of jobs they have, how much money we think they make based on there profession, how an individual looks, where an individual lives, and how they make us feel. When we base our relationships on superficial reasons we tend to change when the circumstances change. We can come up with all kind of excuses to run out because the relationship was not built on a solid foundation. We tell others and ourselves " life is to short to be tripping, I just want to be happy, God does not desire us to live like this, and I may be wrong for running out but God will love me and forgive me anyway", not admitting our motives were not good from the beginning. When the spirit of pride has taken root in our hearts we do not accept responsibility for our actions and we do not take accountability for decisions we make. If we do not recognize the spirit of pride when he comes into our lives, we just may find ourselves booted out of everything we elevate higher than the Creator himself, just as satan was booted out of Heaven because of his selfish and prideful attitude of trying to elevate himself higher than his Creator.

The Spirit of Anger

The spirit of anger comes into our lives to put enmity between us. The spirit of anger ruins more Christian testimonies than any other kind of sin. The spirit of anger occupies the bodies of those persons who keep a record in their minds of the wrongs that have been done to them. The spirit of anger occupies the bodies of those persons who do not want to forgive. **The spirit of anger has many hidden disguises.**

Bitterness

This form of anger causes some of us to regret decisions we have made that turned out to be hurting for us when we have not dealt with our hurtful experiences. One of my co-workers told a story of how he entered into marriage while young and went off to the service. While he was away fighting for his country, he said, "my wife was at home tearing up the country sleeping around." When he returned home his wife was carrying another man's child. He became very bitter and not only did he erase from his mind the four years he was married to his wife, but also four years of his life that was associated with that part of his life. He inflicted his bitterness upon every women he entered into a relationship with, when he felt himself becoming "too close". He was afraid to get close to anyone because of what had happened to him in his first marriage. At some point in his life he remarried, but this marriage was based on a lie. He was not able to admit to his second wife that he had been married before and what caused his first marriage to end in divorce. He lied about his age that was associated with the time he was married to his first wife from the beginning of his marriage to his second wife, and he lived in his marriage inflicting his bitterness on his wife. He would not sleep with his wife, make love to his wife, talk to his wife for weeks at a time, or go anywhere with his wife. He could not see that he was allowing the spirit of anger to occupy his body and use him in his marriage to his second wife.

Unfortunately his second marriage ended in divorce because he never came to grips with his past. Because he was a likable person and a good friend to his friends, he did not see himself as bitter. It was still hurting for him to live with the fact that his first wife had actually gotten pregnant by another man while they were married.

Unforgiveness

This form of anger causes us to resent individuals for causing us pain. The spirit of unforgiveness causes us to sit back and wait for what we believe is the perfect opportunity to seek some type of revenge upon individuals that have put us through painful experiences. The spirit of unforgiveness causes us to have hard feelings toward one another.

I know this married couple and they both cheated on each other in their marriage. At some point in their marriage, both of them got caught. This couple admitted they needed Jesus Christ in their lives and they gave their lives to Christ. In the process of trying to work through their marital problems through Christian Counseling, the husband just could not get over his wife cheating although he too had cheated. He held on to the fact that his wife actually slept with another man. He would paint this picture in his mind of some man doing to his wife what he did to someone else's wife and he could not accept that notion. He imagined his wife loving what was done to her just as he wanted to please his lover and he could not deal with it. The husband allowed the spirit of unforgiveness to occupy his body and his married life became unbearable. Unfortunately their marriage was destroyed because deep down the husband was not willing to forgive his wife. Because of his anger, he could not see himself and what he had put his wife through. His anger eventually destroyed him. He admitted that he did not care about what people told him, that God would not forgive him if he could not forgive his wife. All he could see was another man touching on his wife and he had a problem with that.

Envy

This form of anger causes individuals to become jealous and speak evil against one another. Before my friend Louisa got married she was a part of a prayer group with some older women from her church. Through prayer they shared a lot about themselves and all of them became close friends. All of the women in this prayer group were single and one of the things they asked God for was to send men into their lives to become their husbands. Louisa eventually met a man from the church they attended. She began to spend more time with the man she met and less time with her prayer partners, although she continued to be apart of the prayer group. These women who were supposed to be Louisa's friends and prayer partners became envious of her. They began to gossip among themselves about Louisa. They would tell Louisa it was laid on their hearts that she only wanted to get married for sex, that she just wanted a man in her life to take care of her three children, and if she married the man she was courting it would never work. One of the ladies became so jealous that she began to flirt with Louisa's boyfriend and she would come back and tell the other women in the prayer group Louisa's boyfriend is no good because he flirted with her. These old green-eyed monsters allowed the spirit of envy to occupy their bodies. They lost focus and concentrated more on Louisa's relationship with her man as opposed to praying for Louisa. Because they were angry that a man had not come into their lives, they destroyed there relationship with Louisa and ruined their testimony.

Holding Grudges

This form of anger causes individuals to keep a record in their minds of the wrongs that have been done to them. Larry was a walking time bomb just waiting to go off on somebody. He did not care who just as long as he could let off some steam. He kept a record of girlfriends that broke up with him for no apparent reason, those that "piss him off" as he put it, and those that made him look bad. He was angry because the right opportunity had not presented itself for him to get back at those individuals that were recorded in his book for revenge. Every time he tried to seek revenge on someone that was recorded in his record book it would backfire on him. Larry ended up looking like the bad guy. Because Larry was an angry man, he lived most of adult life planning and waiting for opportunities to seek some type of revenge that never took place. He never came to grips with the fact that he was allowing the spirit of anger to rule his life and occupy his body. He believed, according to Larry, that it was doing unto others as they had done unto him.

Misery

This form of anger causes individuals to try and come up with ways to make others feel as bad as they feel. One of my co-workers would call his wife everyday harassing her while she was at work. We would hear him ask his wife "who did you go to lunch with, did you and your girlfriends booty bump at lunch, how many men did you flirt with today, are you sitting with your legs open." This man became obsessed with harassing his wife and verbally abusing her while she was at work. It got so bad that he was asked not to make any more personal phone calls at work unless it was an emergency. He was disturbing other employees with his abuse to his wife. This man was a miserable creature. Because he was a newly married man we could not understand why he was treating his wife so terribly. Some of us in the department decided we would go to our co-worker and try to minister to him. This man was younger than his wife by 9 years. He felt bad because his wife made more money than he did, she was educated and he was not, she worked out and kept her body in shape, and she treated him good in spite of the way he treated her. He was miserable because she had lots of friends and he did not. He was lazy about working out and jealous of his wife because she was disciplined enough to work-out. Although he was younger, his body sagged and he had very little energy. This man thought that if he could make his wife feel as bad as he felt just maybe she would give up and settle as he felt he had. He did not have the energy to do no more than he was doing because the spirit of misery was zapping his energy. This spirit had consumed this individual. He also felt that his wife would soon leave him for someone that had the same spirit and get-up-and-go as she did. He was miserable because the meaner he treated her the kinder she was to him.

When we allow ourselves to be used by the many disguises of anger we become unemotional and unfeeling. The spirit of anger causes our whole disposition to change so that we are no longer ourselves. We become difficult and unpleasant to be around. We make rash decisions, embarrassing decisions, and harmful decisions because we do not care anymore.

The struggles we experience when the spirit of anger is occupying our bodies grieves the Holy Spirit of God. (Ephesians 4:29-32, KJV) tells us that we grieve the Holy Spirit of God through bitterness, wrath, anger, clamors, evil speaking, and malice which is enmity of heart. This spirit causes our hearts to become hardened and we live together in our marriage as enemies. This spirit causes us to detach ourselves emotionally and we completely shut down. If we do not recognize the many disguises of anger we will eventually destroy ourselves.

The Spirit of Hate

The spirit of hate causes our hearts to become cold blooded. This spirit occupies the bodies of those persons who have allowed the spirit of anger, and its many disguises to take root in their hearts. The spirit of hate has many hidden disguises.

Lynching

This form of hate causes individuals to plan to commit murders. Sin is never committed spontaneously. Before the acts of murder takes place hatred, anger, and bitterness has occupied the bodies and harbored in the hearts. I am reminded of a beautiful lady who was murdered by her husband. This couple had been married for 25 years and in the marriage five children were born. At some point in their marriage a separation took place because the husband was very abusive. According to the husband he was angry and began to feel hate towards his wife because he felt as if his wife had abandoned him. This man had planned his wife's murder. He knew he was going to break into his wife's house and wait for her to return home because he knew her schedule. He knew when she walked inside her house he was going to locked the door and strike her repeatedly over the head with an iron rod until she feel dead. This man knew he wanted to beat his wife's brains out. What a shame, this old man allowed the spirit of hate to occupy his body to the point where he was no longer himself for a split second. A wife that had given him 25 years of marriage and five children he murdered because he allowed the spirit of hate to occupy his body.

Killing

This form of hate causes individuals to deprive others of life. This spirit causes individuals to kill for no apparent reason. We lose many of our future leaders to this form of hate. A lot of our future leaders are growing up with no sense of Christ in their lives and killing themselves slowly by their life-styles. They are giving their lives to the enemy by getting involved in gangs, selling drugs, taking drugs, carrying weapons, and dropping out of school. These drugs are spirits that brings with them strongholds to keep individuals in bondage to them. The spirit of killing is a normal function for gang bangers and drug dealers who do not have Jesus Christ in their lives. The enemy desires our future leaders to grow up confused and without integrity. There is so much in this world to distract our teenagers and the enemy know just what to put before them. We cannot expect our teenagers to be strong enough to stand against the strategies of the enemy if we are not praying for them, loving them, listening to them, teaching them, directing them, and spending quality time with them, finding out what they are doing and thinking. As adults we can find ourselves caught up in some of the same struggles that our teenagers face. We should not expect our teenagers to walk the straight and narrow path when they see us as adults walking the downward and crowded path. Parents are the only role models children know until they come to know Jesus Christ for themselves through their own personal experience.

Stealing

This form of hate causes us to take what belongs to someone else, to mooch off others, and to rob others. It is a crime and a shame when a man steals from his own family. I know a man that would steal from his wife and children. For some reason, this man just could not keep a job, but he wanted the finer things in life. While his wife went to work everyday, he would sit at home eating up everything in the house getting big as the state in which they lived, and he was not contributing a penny to the household. This man had expensive habits for someone who did not work. He would cook up the food his wife would buy for the family and invite his hungry friends over to eat. He loved to drink expensive alcohol. He wanted to wear name brand clothes and would brag about how much his clothes cost. He loved to go clubbing and would buy other folks drinks knowing he did not have a job. His wife finally decided she was going to stop supporting him and insisted that he keep a job. This man became angry and allowed the spirit of hate to occupy his body and began to steal from his hardworking wife and children. He took his own baby's diamond earrings from her ears and pawned them because he was desperate for money. He would pawn whatever he could to support his drinking habit. He became so desperate he probably would have pawned his children if he thought he could get away with it. It got so bad that his wife had to hide her purse, her credit cards, and her check books just to keep her husband from stealing from her. This man not only stole from his wife and children but also mooched off his friends also.

He was always borrowing money from his friends knowing he could not pay them back, wanting to borrow their cars, and hanging out at his so-called friends houses to get whatever they had he liked. This is what the spirit of hate reduces us to when we are not productive in this life here on earth.

Prejudice

This form of hate causes us to become narrow minded in our thinking. We are faced with this spirit every single day of our lives. We see this form of hate among different races of people, among the same race of people, on our jobs, within our families, and among those who profess to be Christians and Saved. The spirit of prejudice has caused individuals to raise up racist hate groups to teach prejudice and race superiority. It is a way of life for these racist hate-groups to practice hatred out of ignorance and inflict hateful acts upon individuals whom are different.

I can remember when I was younger having to always look over my shoulder, afraid to walk home from school by myself for fear of being attacked by racist individuals. These individuals would let their dogs loose to attack those of us walking home from school. Lord knows we were called everything but children of God. The bad part about all of this is, these were adults allowing the spirit of hate to occupy their bodies to attack children. Some of these racist hate groups covered themselves. They did not want to be uncovered just as these evil spirits that we fight against daily desire to stay covered. Because of our ignorance to the spirit of prejudice we find ourselves caught up in many struggles that we bring on ourselves.

We do understand that this spirit exists but that does not stop us from dating the enemy, marrying the enemy, adopting the ways of the enemy, trying to be like the enemy, and thinking like the enemy. The spirit of hate today is destroying many people, has destroyed many people, many organizations, many homes, and many families. It exists now and will continue to exist long after we have slipped from time into eternity.

Despise

This form of hate causes us to condemn others. It can hinder us from drawing others to Christ. Sophia was scorned by her family and friends because her husband walked off and left her. Her friends and family wanted to know what Sophia did to cause her husband to leave her after six months of marriage. Most people saw Sofia's husband as a good Christian man because he worked so diligently in the church. He was a good Sunday School teacher, he went to Bible Study, and he was a hard working deacon. Sofia's family and friends told her she had caused her husband to leave her because she was too "outspoken, harsh, loud, and confrontational, which are not the qualities of a Godly Christian woman." Sofia was hurt because her family and friends, who had known her a lot longer than they had known her husband, had judged her and found her guilty. Sofia may have been some of those things in the past but she had changed. In the eyes of her family and friends she was out of the Will of God.

We can be so quick to condemn others without even knowing the facts. It was good that Sofia knew who she was in Christ. Sofia did not allow the spirit of despise to occupy her body to cause her to hate her family and friends for judging her. In the end, Sofia's husband came back. He admitted he had some issues he needed to work through to become the husband God wanted him to be to Sofia. Sofia's family and friends recognized their qualities were not Godly because they had judged Sofia's situation instead of praying for her situation.

When we allow ourselves to be used by the spirit of hate, we will speak mean and cruel to each other. The spirit of hate causes individuals to kill for no reason and to despise others who are different from them. The spirit of hate has burned down church buildings, locked up innocent people, torn up families, hanged individuals, stolen from individuals, cheated individuals, plotted against individuals, taken the credit for what someone else has accomplished, and mobbed individuals. This spirit of hate causes resentment between nations, among races of people, among families, among neighbors, among co-workers, and among the saints of God.

The struggles we have when the spirit of hate is occupying our bodies, are the breaking of law and order. We become very destructive in the way we live our lives. We will walk around here on earth as if we live in a world by ourselves doing whatever this spirit put in our minds to do. We will physically fight. We will argue every time we try to communicate. We will curse each other.

The Spirit of Fear

The spirit of fear comes into our lives to stop us in our tracks. This spirit occupies the bodies of those persons who put their trust in man and in themselves. The spirit of fear, like the spirit of anger, and the spirit of hate, has many hidden disguises. Some of the many hidden disguise of the spirit of fear are:

Suspicion

This form of fear causes us to live on the edge, suspicious of others and worried about what other individuals are thinking about us. Mikel would question everything someone said or asked him concerning his family. He was afraid that someone would find out just how he was living in his marriage. Mikel did not want his wife to talk on the phone, have friends over to their house, and he wanted her to be mindful of what she said to others at their church. Mikel begged his wife to marry him, but when they got married he lived with his wife as if they were roommates. Mikel knew that others would see the way he was living in his marriage as odd. Mikel feared that he would be looked upon as crooked or homosexual if his wife talked about the way they were living. The way Mikel lived with his wife went against not only the teachings of the word of our Father but also the teachings of his pastor concerning marriage. Mikel was trying to live celibate in his marriage and feared that someone would find out. Thank God Mikel finally got some help for his problems before he allowed his marriage to be destroyed. Once Mikel truly gave his problem to our Father, he could finally admit to his wife that for a long time masturbation had taken the place of him having a woman in his life. He thought that his wife would see him as being queer, therefore he could not discuss this problem with her at first. He was trying to live a Godly life by not sleeping around and he did not want any babies outside of marriage, so he would masterbate. Mikel was feeling guilty because he made his wife believe that he had been celibate before he married her, but deep within, he felt as if he had been in a relationship with some evil spirit because of his masturbating.

Worry

This form of fear causes us to become consumed by things we have no control over. Most of what we stress ourselves about never happens the way we perceive it in our minds because we cannot predict what our Father will allow. This is why we are instructed to give everything we desire over to our Father and let Him work out our cares and concerns because worrying is a sin that causes us to be tired and stressed out.

Before I began to mature in the word of God I was very fearful about death. It bothered me when someone I knew died especially if they were young. I can remember trying to stay up all night scared to sleep. I thought if I could just keep my eyes open, I had a better chance of not dying. I would go days trying to stay awake at night with no sleep. The lack of sleep caused me to be irritable, have dark circles under my eyes, walk around like a zombie, and feel tired. I felt trapped because I had no inner peace. Little did I know at the time that the spirit of fear was occupying my body and causing me to worry about something I had no control of anyway. As I began to pray more about my fear of death, eventually, my worries went away. I found myself laying down at night sleeping very peaceful.

Cowardice

This form of fear causes us to act like cowards when we go along to get along as opposed to standing for what is true. The spirit of cowardice keeps us from stepping up and taking our roles our Father has given us.

Jeremy lived with his mother until he was 35 years old. He went from his mom's house to his wife's home. Whenever Jeremy had a problem with his wife he would run home to his mom for advice. Jeremy always did what his mom told him to do as opposed to communicating with his wife. The advice Jeremy got from his mom was not always sound for the difficulties he and his wife were having at the time. During holiday get-togethers Jeremy's mom would try to "run things" and refused to support his wife which always caused a struggle in their home. Jeremy was afraid to tell his mom to back off although he knew deep within that she was wrong. During Jeremy's marriage to his wife he bought his mom a house and he and his wife lived in a cramped apartment. Jeremy traded his car in and bought his mom a car and he and his wife shared her car. He argued that his wife was ungrateful and defended his mother's interferences. It is unfortunate that Jeremy's marriage ended in divorce because he never stepped up and took his place as a husband. Jeremy allowed the spirit of cowardice to occupy his body to the point where he could not tell his mother to back off in a loving way. Jeremy blamed his wife for the things that went wrong in their marriage and eventually went back to live with his mother.

Doubt

This form of fear keeps us from doing what our Father instructs us to do. We find ourselves taking matters into our own hands and taking back from our Father what we asked Him to do for us through prayer.

It was rumored that this particular company was getting ready to lay off some of their employees. The rumor did not seem to bother those who had been with the company for an extended period of time. One employee in particular that comes to my mind was a youth minister who told his department he was praying for the company and the word of God tells us to be submissive to those in authority over us. His famous words were "this is the real world and you got to know how to play the games." As far as we could see this youth minister was the only one in the department politicking. He started going to happy hour with those that he would say you don't want to piss off because these individuals had a lot to do with who was going to be laid off. But of course, he was ministering to his bosses while they got their drinks on and while he sipped on virgin drinks. Going to happy hour was a part of him being submissive to those in authority over him. He even began to snitch on some of the workers, which was also a part of him being submissive to those in authority over him. This youth minister seem to have forgotten who placed him in the position he was in. He allowed the spirit of doubt to occupy his body to trust in his bosses as opposed to trusting in the One who gave him the position. This youth minister sold his soul to the devil for a time just to keep his job and he was the only employee that got laid off.

The spirit of fear causes us to be anxious and our peace is taken away. We can become susceptible to all kinds of problems when fear occupies our bodies. Emotional problems, multiple personalities, physical ailments, mental anguish, and fear can bring on some type of diseases in our bodies. The spirit of fear keeps us from moving forward in this life while we are here on earth and we do not reach our full potential. We find ourselves going through life doing just enough to get by limiting ourselves and not growing because we are afraid to step out on faith.

When we allow ourselves to be used by the spirit of fear, our hearts becomes spiritless. We find ourselves stressed out because we worry about our jobs, worry about money, worry about our health, worry about what people say and think of us, worry about what people try to plot against us as opposed to trusting our Father. All these worries that the spirit of fear puts into our mind causes us to become depressed because we are trying to cope with the many disguises of fear with our own strength.

The struggles we have when the spirit of fear is occupying our bodies are quenching the Holy Spirit of God. When we quench the Holy Spirit through the many disguises of fear, it keeps us from being effective in this life while we are here on earth, and steal many rewards in the life to come. The spirit of fear causes us to give in to the enemy and be defeated. Our biggest struggles with the spirit of fear is not trusting our Father for our battles that we face in this life down here on earth.

The Spirit of Rebellion

The spirit of rebellion is the root and essence of sin. This spirit occupies the bodies of those who want to have their way at any cost and those who do not want to listen. The spirit of rebellion occupies the bodies of those who have not learned from their mistakes of the past because they did not hear. Sin entered this cosmos when satan rebelled against our Father. (See Isaiah 14:12-17, KJV). Sin entered the human body when Adam rebelled against Gods word. (See Genesis 3, KJV).

When we allow ourselves to be used by the spirit of rebellion, we willfully become disobedient to the word of our Father. The spirit of rebellion causes us to do just what we feel big and bad enough to do.

I know a man who was married to a person whose job required a lot of traveling. The wife made more money than her husband and it began to agitate the man. He began to feel less than a man because his wife was making most of their money. He knew before he married his wife what kind of money she made but after he married her, he could not handle it. He began to allow the spirit of rebellion to occupy his body. He stopped communicating with his wife, he stopped making love to his wife, and he would tell his wife "don't touch me." He would tell his wife to do what she wanted to do and to let God deal with him. In the process of his acting like a child, he never stopped teaching Sunday School, he never stopped ushering, he never stopped evangelizing, and he never stopped studying the word of God. This man waited until his wife went on a business trip to move out of their home. He took everything and told his wife she could afford to start over. The wife never gave up on her husband. She loved him and understood what he was going through. She kept praying for her husband. She could recognize that her husband was allowing the spirit of rebellion to occupy his body. Her prayers were answered. Her husband came back. He realized himself that he was rebelling against God and allowing satan to steal his blessings.

The struggles we have when the spirit of rebellion is occupying our bodies is living carnal lives. A carnal person is one whose actions lust after the things of this world. Lot's wife is a good example of rebellion. She is called the mother of rebellion. (See Luke 17:23, KJV). The spirit of rebellion will lead us to our doom as in the case of Lots wife.

The Spirit of Deception

The spirit of deception deceives us by causing us to believe we are right when we are wrong. The spirit of deception occupies the bodies of those persons who profess to be saved but are not committed. The spirit of deception occupies the bodies of those who have not come to grips with the fact that they cannot fool God our Father. The spirit of deception causes these persons to sit in deception thinking they are fooling others, but in reality deception has them fooled. The spirit of deception knows just what to say to someone who is moved by what they hear, knows the look to send someone who is moved by what they see, and knows how to treat someone who is moved by their feelings. The spirit of deception is the same spirit that appeared to Eve in the Garden of Eden as an angel of light. (See II Corinthians 13, KJV). The spirit of deception can be so convincing that God's chosen people can be deceived for a time.

The following is a sad story about a person who was deceived by the man she thought was her husband. She had dated this man for a year and felt that she knew him well enough to marry him. She went to an apartment that she believed was his because she spent numerous nights with him there. He told her he was 35 years old and she believed him. She did not have any reason to question his age. He told her he had never been married and she believed him. He told her he did not have any children and she believed him. He told her he did construction work for a living and she believed him. He also told her one day he was going to take her to his country and she believed him. After two years of marriage a woman and four children showed up at their apartment with their belongings. This person that showed up was also married to this man. She was his wife from his native country. This man had ruined another person's life by deceiving her. She was married to a man that was already married with four children. His name was totally different from what she knew his name to be and he was much older than what he admitted to being. This man deceived this person because he knew he could not have her if she knew that in his country he could have more than one wife. He also understood that in our country it is against the law to be married to more than one wife. This man was planning to take his wife to his country and force her to accept his marriage to his first wife and his four children from his country. His mission was not accomplished. He never got the chance because his family came to him unexpected. He did not get away with trying to deceive the other person he was married to. At some point in our lives, that which is hidden will be manifested because it is Written and our Father cannot lie.

When we allow ourselves to be used by the spirit of deception, we perpetrate, by pretending to be someone or something we are not. We can find ourselves working in the church building for all the wrong reasons, lying for no apparent reason, and saying just what we believe someone wants to hear.

The struggles we have, when the spirit of deception is occupying our bodies, is not knowing the person we are dealing with or living with. It is very difficult to live a lie. At some point, the real spirit of the person we are dealing with or living with, is going to come to the forefront and remain consistent. The spirit of deception causes us to go through life not understanding life as it really is because we are not being our true selves.

Our struggles while we are here on earth are battles with the unseen. These battles started in Heaven long before the foundation of this earth age; a battle between the Holy Angels of God who stood-against satan, and those angels that stood-along with satan, a battle between the forces of good and the forces of evil, a battle between unfallen and fallen angels. Although we cannot perceive these spirits with our corporeal eyes they are here on this earth. (See Revelation 12:7-9, KJV).

While here on earth these battles are within each of us. A battle between the children of God and the children of satan. (See Genesis 3:15, KJV). We fight with the spirits that each of us allow to occupy our bodies, which causes us to struggle. These old evil spirits try to keep us from receiving our blessings while here on earth by causing confusion in our lives, trying to keep us from understanding and doing what we are instructed to do. We find ourselves blaming each other for our actions, not recognizing the evil force behind the person we are fighting. These old evil spirits also try to keep our blessings from reaching us here on earth. These evil spirits are persistent at trying to defeat us in this life. When we can recognize the spirit of the enemy and do what we are instructed to do by our Father, without trying to put logic to it and complaining, satan is mad because his goals were not accomplished. These evil spirits will try to attack God's messengers to keep them from getting our blessings to to us. Daniel was a man that was beloved by God. It is written in Daniel Chapter 10:11- 13, KJV how Daniel's prayers were heard and answered by God. The angel of God that was sent to give Daniel an understanding of what would happen to his people (the Jews) in "the latter days" was confronted by the enemy and was held up for 21 days. Daniel was a man of great faith. He did not allow anyone to tell him that God had already answered His prayers and his answer was no. Daniel's faith caused him to wait on God. Daniel did not realize the angels of God were in a three-week spiritual battle described by a holy angel of God. A lesson for us as believers is that God's Will for us on earth will be done in our lives, regardless of how difficult our struggles may appear. Also when we are praying about something in our lives and it seems as if God is taking a long time to answer our prayers, maybe our angel is up in Heaven fighting the enemy on our behalf. It is important that we do not give up. We must continue to trust God and stand on His promises in spite of how ever long we may feel we have been waiting. It is important that we keep in mind our Father knows when we are ready to handle the things we ask for in prayer.

Every struggle we face in this life while here on earth our Father knows, He cares about, and He allows them to be. Satan cannot do anything to the Saints of God that our Father does not allow. As a matter of fact, satan has to get permission from our Father when dealing with His Saints as in the case of Job. (See Job Chapter 1, KJV). When these evil spirits are allowed to come into our lives we are not being tempted with evil. We are being put to a test in order for us to know for ourselves if we are ready for our specific purpose while here on earth. We begin to know things about ourselves that our Father already knows about us when we are going through our struggles. We become more aware of our weaknesses and whose we are when going through our struggles. Temptation comes when we stop trusting our Father and begin to handle our struggles with our fleshly weapons. (See James 1:13-14, KJV).

Because each of us has a specific purpose while here on earth our Father allows us to go through struggles for many different reasons. There are times in our lives, the reasons for our struggles are made known to us while going through them. There are times in our lives, the reasons for our struggles are not made known to us until after we have stood in our struggles, by trusting our Father. There are times in our lives, the reasons for our struggles are not made known to us at all. Only our Father knows before we go into our struggles the reasons why He is allowing them to be. If we were never allowed by our Father to go through any struggles we would not have any testimonies. We would not be able to handle our blessings. We would not be equipped for our specific purpose while here on earth neither would we mature spiritually. In other words, we would not survive in the life here on earth. We should see our struggles as a blessing from our Father, no matter how difficult they may appear to be. It is a confirmation that our Father has a purpose for us that was determined before the foundation of this earth age. It is a confirmation that we belong to Him. It is a confirmation that he loves us enough to take us through a fire without getting burned in order for us to gain spiritual muscles to be used for His Glory, while here on earth. But we must stand in our struggles, trusting Him.

A lot of struggles we encounter in this life while here on earth are struggles we bring on ourselves. Most of the time these evil spirits come into our lives and occupy our bodies because we allow them, by doing just what we feel big and bad enough to do. We justify our actions by saying, " I'm grown and I can do whatever I want to do." As we mature spiritually, we should understand that we cannot do whatever we want to do outside the Will of God. When we adopt this attitude and begin to live our lives accordingly, we are definitely allowing the evil spirits of satan to rule our lives.

When we put our jobs before God and our families, we are allowing ourselves to be used by the enemy, and we have just brought a struggle on ourselves. Our Father is not pleased and our homes are not happy. When we put our jobs before God and our families, this causes unnecessary stress in our lives that we have brought on ourselves. We are slowly killing ourselves. Some of us are taking all kinds of different medication because we are letting our jobs stress us. Some of us have had heart attacks, strokes, and high blood pressure because we are going along with the enemy to stay on that particular job. We are stressing because deep down we know that this is out of God's order. We fear that if we tell the enemies how we really feel we just might lose our jobs. The enemy does not care about us giving time to our Father and our families. When we kill ourselves as a result of trusting our enemies on our jobs, nothing much will be said besides " we worked ourselves to death and we let our jobs stress us out." My brothers and sisters we have got to keep in our minds, what our Father has given us no man can take away from us. If our Father allows our jobs to be taken away from us, He definitely has another job waiting around the corner that is better for us There are times in our lives the very things that we put before our Father and our families, are the things that He allows to be taken away from us in order that we can come to grips with what we are doing. Putting other gods before Him, which is our jobs.

When we try to put someone down on our jobs to make ourselves look good, or to get a promotion, it causes a struggle that we have brought on ourselves. When we believe in our minds we have to "kiss up booty" to get a promotion, we must understand the promotion was not really earned. This type of struggle can cause individuals to be burden down and stressed. These individuals will never know on a day to day basis what craziness the enemy will want them to perform just to keep their jobs. You had better believe the enemy will expect these individuals to allow themselves to be used by him, to accomplish his goals on the job. The enemy gives temporary blessing that appears to be offers that can't be refused. When the enemy cannot use these individuals anymore, he can cause these individuals to appear as troubles makers, individuals that are not team players, and individuals who are incompetent to take back what he gave them. What a hell of a price to pay just to get a promotion.

When we bring someone into our lives knowing we are angry, knowing we do not care for ourselves, knowing we have not dealt with our experiences of the past, we have just brought a struggle into someone else's life. We cannot give to others what we do not have inside of us to give. We cannot care for others when we do not care for ourselves. We cannot understand another person when we lack understanding. Dealing with our struggles through faith in God causes us to understand life and how it really is for us while we are here on earth.

When parents are not teaching their children and they are still given everything they lust after, it causes them to struggle in life. They grow up being little idolators not understanding the value of a dollar. They grow up not understanding real responsibility. They grow up thinking they can have anything they want. They grow up not being prepared to function in this life down here on earth. Some of these individuals will not survive if they do not come to know Jesus Christ for themselves through their own personal experiences. Some of these individuals will turn to stealing, cheating, and drugs when they cannot get what they lust after. Some of these individuals will grow up hurting, killing, and shaming their families when they cannot get what they lust after. All these situations cause them to struggle in life because the instructions our Father left were not carried out.

When we enter into a marriage for all the wrong reasons, it causes a struggle that we have brought on ourselves and others. We could possibly be with a person that was meant for someone else. We mess up someone else's life that is sincerely trying to commit to our Father in their marriage. If a divorce come about as a result of someone marrying for all the wrong reasons, we have to deal with the fact that what we shared with our mates are now being shared with someone else. We have to deal with starting over and getting back what we had before we entered into this marriage. Sometimes we have to deal with our credit being ruined as result of having to start over when a separation takes place. These are unnecessary struggles that we have brought on ourselves and others because someone was not for real when they took their marriage vows.

When we say our Father called us to do something and he did not call us to do what we are claiming, it causes a struggle that we have brought on ourselves. We stand before God's people looking stupid, sounding stupid, and being misunderstood. We find ourselves struggling when we are doing what we want to do with no direction from our Father. We find ourselves struggling when we are doing what we believe is popular at the time. We find ourselves struggling when we not being our true selves in order that we may know our true calling or specific purpose while here on earth. Our Father does not want us stumbling because we represent Him in this world. When we are called out for a specific purpose our Father first prepares us to go before His people. (See Romans 8:29, KJV). We will speak boldly with confidence and grace. We will know what we are talking about and we will be understood.

When we sit back meddling in other folk's affairs, gossiping about things we do not know anything about, it causes a struggle that we have brought on ourselves. We lose sight of what we should be doing because we are caught up in what someone else is doing. These individuals who are being gossiped about are going on with their lives. Meddling in other folks affairs not only causes us to struggle but we also suffer some consequences when we gossip about individuals we know nothing about. We never know if we are meddling with someone that belongs to satan, or someone that belongs to our Father. Satan protects his own, just as our Father, protects His own. When we are gossiping about someone that belongs to satan we could possibly get sued, beat up, hurt, or killed. When someone messes with a child of God it is also very dangerous. When someone strike one of His, try to destroy one of His, and spread rumors on one of His, God deals with them. It is written, "touch not mine anointed." (See I Chronicles 16:22, KJV). We must remember our Father's word will not come back to Him void.

Relationships based on sex outside of marriage cause struggles that we have brought on ourselves. We can find ourselves caught up in many types of bad situations; pregnancy outside of marriage, giving ourselves to someone who does not want to commit, settling for less than what our Father desires us to have, sometimes contracting sexually transmitted diseases, dealing with fatal attractions, giving what belongs to the person our Father has for us to someone else, sleeping with the enemy, and wasting our valuable time.

In situations where we allow the enemy into our lives, we are definitely going to struggle. In these type struggles we will have no peace in our lives until we decide to boot the enemy out of our lives. When we have brought a struggle on ourselves by allowing the enemy to come into our lives and we know better, our Father is not going to make us do what we already know as the right thing to do. These evil spirits are here so we can know the difference between right, wrong, good, evil, and to choose between them. As a matter of fact, our Father tells us there will be no peace for those of us who willingly allow the enemy into our lives. There will be no peace for those of us that cause others to struggle as a result of us allowing ourselves to be used by the enemy. (See Isaiah 48:22, KJV). We will not only have no peace but we will also have to pay for the bad choices we made that was wrong or evil.

Some of these struggles we bring on ourselves causes us to be torn down, worn down, broken down, burden down, used up, and tired from ducking, dodging, hiding, and lying. A life filled with drama and confusion is what we have when we allow ourselves to be used by the enemy. Some of us even have the nerve to say, "we are praying that God show us what to do in our struggles," when we willingly invite the enemy into our lives. The enemy cause us to believe our Holy Father is in the midst of our unholy mess. We are supposed to take everything to our Father in prayer. But when we purposefully play around with the enemy we are not being faithful. The Holy Angels of God do not play around with satan even with the awesome power they have and neither should we. We can boot the enemy out of our lives by simply telling him no and meaning "no" in the name of Jesus.

Struggles we bring on ourselves causes us to know

A. That which is hidden will be manifested
B. What is done in the dark will come to the light
C. When we do not do things right it will not work out right
D. The same people we dogged out moving up will be the same people to see us when we fall
E. God our Father does not forget, He will deal with us for choices we made
F. We reap what we sow and it is worse
G. When we tell a lie, we have to tell another one to cover the first one, and pretty soon our life is one big lie
H. We have been used
I. What is good to us for the moment is not always good for us in the long
J. We are no match for the enemy without the power of God
K. We have been fooled

When we are in a struggle for righteousness sake our Father is pleased. When we trust him through our struggles we are being shaped into the image He wants for us. In this type of struggle others can see the power of God working in our lives. In this type of struggle others can be blessed by our experiences. The struggles our Father allows us to go through while we are here on earth are necessary in order that we may be delivered from eternal suffering. When we are in a struggle it doesn't necessarily mean we have been bad just as not having struggles doesn't mean that we have been so good. As we go through our struggles and continue to obey the Word of our Father we are rewarded in the end for trusting Him.

It was a blessing to me to watch this friend of mine stand against the forces of satan during a difficult time in his marriage. His wife had just had her third child when she took sick. He was forced to take care of a newborn baby and two other children along with caring for his sick wife, who could not work at the time because of her sickness. His company went through a merger and he was one of the employees that was laid off from work. I remember this friend of mine praising God for his struggles during Bible study. I remember him praising God for being laid off his job because it gave him more time to spend with his newborn baby, his other children, and his sick wife. I can still see him walking into our Bible study class as if a burden had been lifted off of him with his children giving testimonies. He knew God had allowed him to be laid off because he had something better for him. Because he had a good technical background working with computers; he was able to start his own business at home which was computer consulting and building computers. He made more money working at home and he was able to spend more time with his family. My friend did not allow the forces of satan to use him to get angry about his situation. He saw his struggle as a blessing in disguise. He put his trust in God and he was blessed tremendously. It was refreshing to know there are still individuals here on earth that will not sell their soul to the devil by politicking, scheming, lying, and killing themselves just to keep a certain job.

Struggles We Face When We Struggle For Right Allows Us To Know

A. Who we belong To
B. Our Faith
C. If We Can Stand
D. Who we Trust While going Through our Struggles
E. How Committed We Are
F. God Cannot Lie and His Word Does Not Come Back To Void
G. God is Real
H. How Much We Love God our Father
I. How Real We Are
J. Spiritual Warfare
K. Patience

It is one thing for us to say what we will and will not do, how we would be, what we can tolerate, what we can and will not put up with, but we really do not know until we have actually experienced it through our struggles. We are in no position to tell someone to "hang in there" if we've never experienced obstacles ourselves. We are in no position to tell someone to leave a struggle that we have not gone through ourselves. We are in no position to tell someone how they should act while going through their struggles if we have not been there ourselves. Because we do not have the mind of our Father we should not try to tell someone what God's Will is for them as they go through struggles. When we take it upon ourselves to advise someone of what they should do, we better make sure we are being directed by our Father to do so. We can always advise someone to pray that God show him or her what His Will is for them as they go through their struggles. We can find ourselves dealing with struggles we never imagined we could deal with. We can find ourselves running from struggles when we believed ourselves to be strong. Only God knows what we are capable of handling and not handling. When our Father allows us to go through a struggle he already knows that we can deal with whatever He allows. He knows how we are going to deal with what He allows. He knows if we will deal with what He allows. Our Father knows each and every one of his children. He knows every struggle we are dealing with right now and every struggle we will encounter in the future. He knows what type of struggle He need to allow each of us to go through, to get us to the point where we need to be for our specific purpose or calling while here on earth.

The struggles that our Father allows us to go through should develop us and not destroy us, mature us and not cripple us. The struggles our Father allows us to go through are supposed to shape us up and not tear us down, teach us and not blind us. The struggles our Father allows us to go through are supposed to prepare us for what our Father has in store for us. Our struggles are necessary in order that we can be who and what our Father desires us to be for His glory.

Satan, our enemy, uses struggles to destroy and our Father can turn into victories when we trust him. There are times our Father uses these fallen angels to accomplish certain tasks in order that His plan will be fulfilled. Lying spirits were used in the mouths of the prophets of Ahab, the King of Israel, in order that he might fall at Ramoth Gilead and fulfill God's purpose. (See I Kings 22:19-22, KJV). The evil spirit of the Lord tormented Saul because he had been rejected by God to become King over Israel in order that David would be brought to the court of Saul, among the people he would ultimately rule over, and thus God's purpose was fulfilled. (See I Samuel 16:14-22-23, KJV). Satan and his many evil forces are used to perfect us in many ways. Each time satan along with his many evil forces come at us, and the more we trust our Father, we are being perfected in areas of our lives. We become our true selves by dealing with our struggles through faith in God. This is the only way we can become our true selves and know whose we are by standing in our struggles and allowing our Father to take full control of our struggles.

When we can recognize satan along with his many evil forces and come together in prayer, all of hell is trembling. The devil is mad again. We have the power to stop any evil spirit that occupy our bodies when they are not welcome into our lives. The only powers satan and his evil forces have are the powers that we give to them, when we allow them to use us and occupy our bodies. As children of God we have more power than these evil forces that we allow into our lives. Our power is that of the Holy Spirit of God dwelling inside of us. The Holy Spirit is more powerful than any evil force satan sends our way because He is God. We must give Him complete control to fight our battles with the unseen.

When we allow our Father to fight our battles for us we come up out of them in our right minds as if we had never been through a struggle. When we can trust our Father while going through our struggles he is proud of each of us as His children. The enemy gets defeated. We can come up out of our struggles better Christians. Amen

Chapter Four

Communication Among The Saints Of God

**Let no corrupt communication proceed out of your mouth,
but that which is good to the use edifying,
that it may minister grace unto the hearer.
Ephesians 4:29, KJV**

The word of God emphasizes over and over how we as believers should communicate with one another. Our words should be encouraging, with the intent of building up one another at all times. Even when we are angry with one another, have to say no to one another, or tell one another how we feel, our words should be graceful. The words that proceed out of our mouths ought to minister so it can be a blessing to the hearer and our Father can be glorified.

Communication is sharing our ideas and thoughts. It not only involves eye contact, body language, facial expressions, listening, understanding what is being said, but also what a person is not saying. Communication skills can be difficult to teach, and that is why it often takes practice and time. Prayer is an awesome way of opening up communication lines. It starts with us getting into the presence of our Father communicating to Him, listening as He speaks to our hearts, understanding what our Father expects from us, and carrying out the responsibilities He has given each of us from His word.

Our first real relationship that we establish should be with our Father in order for us to understand how to communicate right with other individuals. It is impossible to have a relationship with our Father when we do not communicate with Him through prayer. As we go before our Father in prayer and say, "I am a sinner, Lord save me, change my heart, show me your way, lead me in the right way, protect me from my enemies, direct me your way," we are communicating with our Father through prayer. We are establishing a relationship with our Father as we communicate with Him through prayer. In the process, He prepares each of us for our own relationships with other individuals that we come in contact with while here on earth. He teaches us what we did not learn about communication while we were young growing up.

Psalms 50:23, KJV says "Whoso offereth praise glorifieth me; and to him that ordereth his conversation alright will I show the salvation of God". God our Father deserves our praises and desires real, true genuine praise. Because God knows the heart of every man, He knows those of us who are sincere when we are praising Him. He knows those of us who are allowing ourselves to be used by satan just to be praised by man when praising Him.

Our Father loves to be praised. When we say to our Father in prayer, We love you, We worship you, You are almighty, You are all powerful, You are awesome, You are sovereign, You hold this earth together, You are the creator of all of heaven & earth, and You are all Knowing, we are communicating praises to our Father. As we offer sincere praise to our Father, He becomes to each of us all of what we communicate to Him.

Because mankind was made in the image and likeness of our Father we possess some of the same similarities of the divine. Man loves praises and wants to be praised. When we say to our mates, "you are blessed in the Lord, you can do all things through Jesus Christ, you are more than a conqueror, you are strong, you are the head, you got it going on, you are the one," we are communicating praises to our mates and allowing the Spirit of Love to take root in our communication in order to build up our mates. This type of praise is not, a prideful praise. We are encouraging our mates and building them in the process. We are speaking life to our mates, blessing them and constantly reminding them of what they are as our Father causes them to become more like Him. The more we enter into good communication with our loved one we strengthen our relationship because of it's foundation in the Word of God.

Woman loves praises and wants to be praised. When our mates say to us, we are blessed in the Lord, we are appreciated, we are heard, we are understood, we are wanted, we are needed, we are beautiful, and we feel what's communicated is genuine because it is shown by their actions; the Spirit of Submission takes place without understanding it. This type of praise is not a prideful praise. Our mates are encouraging us. We are receiving blessings from our mates. Our mates are covering us with the Word of our Father. We are receiving positive communication from our mates. Life is being spoken to us. We are being constantly reminded that we are the greatest gift our Father ever gave to man. The more our mates provide us with good communication, the more we will reflect those characteristics of a godly woman.

Our Father knows the effect corrupt communication can have on relationships. When we allow ourselves to be used by the spirit of corruptness, it causes us to put down one another, tear down one another, speak harshly to one another, curse one another, speak negatively to one another, and to speak death to one another. We can kill one another with bad communication. When we tell someone to go to hell, or they will never be anything, they are dumb, or worthless, that we do not care for them, or we don't want them around, that they are ugly, or we cannot stand being around them, we are killing them with negative words and allowing ourselves to be used by the many evil forces of satan. When we put each other down to tear down we are really saying to Our Father, "I do not like the way you created that person." We must remember that our Father created each of us unique and special in our own way. The personalities our Father gave each of us and what we become as a result of not communicating or dealing with our experiences are often different. Our true personalities are often hidden when we allow ourselves to be used mightily by

our enemies. Our "for real" personalites manifests when we allow the Spirit of Love to take charge over our lives.

Corrupt Communication

A. Can be a curse
B. Can be a hindrance to someone else
C. Can damage a person's self esteem
D. Causes disrespect
E. Can destroy our marriages
F. Can destroy our fellowship with God
G. Can cause our prayers to be hindered
H. Can cause a struggle that we have brought on ourselves
I. Can cause us to be used mightily by the enemy
J. Can cause us to cripple someone
K. Causes us to be negative
L. Can attack someone's character

Men and women communicate differently. One cannot grow and mature adequately when there is no communication, thinking, and sharing of feelings. Women, for the most part, tend to be more into relationships than most men are. In the beginning when God gave Eve to Adam as his helpmate, Eve came into a relationship with Adam as his wife. They were to be as one, united together in the spirit of our Father. Eve's purpose was to assist her husband. (See Genesis 2:24, KJV). Perhaps this is the reason woman seem to be more into relationships than most men. Most of us as women can usually express ourselves through communication in some way. We tend to be more into studying the word of God in hopes of building better relationships with our spouses. We tend to hang in our marriages even when things are terrible by praying, standing, and waiting on our Father to work out for us any struggle we may be dealing with. We tend to deal with more drama, than most men can deal with professing to be saved and in the church. It's something mighty wrong with this picture.

For the most part, we as women will communicate and do communicate with our mates our needs, what we like, what we dislike, our values, our beliefs, and what we want from our relationships. We definitely want to know from our mates what they like, what they dislike, what their needs are, their values, their beliefs, and the direction in which we are going in our relationships. These are some things we usually ask and discuss early on in our relationships. We do remember most of what is said to us from our mates about our relationships. We do not forget because it is important to us that what has been communicated is being carried out. In order for us to know and understand the person we are in a commitment with, we are supposed to communicate these issuses to one another. Most of the time we find ourselves confused trying to figure these issues out because what was communicated is not being carried out. We then become frustrated because we feel as if we have been deceived in some way. Here we come again reminding our mates of what was said or implied, expressing how we are feeling at the time, communicating what we expect again, and wanting to know what our mates really want. We are sharing our thoughts and our feelings and seeking genuine communication in order to understand the direction in we are going.

Some men, for the most part, tend not to be as communicative as most women are. In the beginning when our Father created Adam, he was giving dominion over the eastward part of the Garden of Eden. The first man formed was a ruler and a conqueror from the very beginning. He had a position first before he was giving Eve as his companion. (See Genesis 2:15, KJV). Adam was a working man and work was all he knew until God gave Eve to Adam as his wife. Prior to Eve becoming Adam's wife, God prepared Adam for this union by teaching Adam how to communicate. Adam's first real relationship was with our Father. Adam walked and talked with God daily. When there is no relationship with our Father all we can do is pray for our mates because the communication will be lacking.

It is difficult for some men to open up and communicate their real feelings, to show emotions, to compromise, to submit, and to really listen with an open heart. When we fail to listen and understand what is being communicated, our relationships suffer. Most of the time we have to learn the hard way by experiencing a lot of struggles that we have brought on ourselves because we are not communicating with one another, we are not listening to what is being communicated, and we are not understanding what is being communicated.

In the process of trying to communicate with one another we have to be mindful that our communication can be up lifting. We have the power of life in our tongues and we have the power to bless. Sometimes this can be a way of getting another individual to open up and communicate with us when we are speaking life to them. When we say to someone, "we love you, we care about you, we respect how you feel, we are here for you, we appreciate you, we want you around", we are blessing them with positive communication. We are speaking life into someone's spirit that may be spiritless. There are a lot of reasons why individuals do not open up and communicate. Only our Father knows. When we are blessed with the ability to be able to communicate, we should always try to encourage others to know they have this same ability. We can encourage others by building them up with good wholesome communication.

Good Communication Brings

A. Wholeness
B. Submission on both parts
C. Excitement
D. Praying Together
E. Oneness
F. Willingness to Please
G. Romance
H. Creativity
I. Togetherness
J. Intimacy
K. Action
L. Respect
I. Order
J. Trust

These are good temperaments the comes from the Spirit of Love that enhances and strengthens our relationships and causes them to stay alive.

Listening is a big part of communication that involves the whole person. When we listen with an open heart we do not try to anticipate what the other person is going to say. We should not finish the other person's sentence for them. We cannot be tuning out what is being said simply because we have a problem with that person. The scripture tells us that we should be quick to listen, talk less, and slow to anger. (See James 1:19, KJV). God requires us to listen to each other. When we are not listening to one another then we are not hearing our Father. When the same things have to be repeated over and over, someone has not listened or understood what was being communicated. When we are not listening to one another it causes us to feel uncared for, unwanted, and unloved. The danger of not listening causes us to become the perfect target for the evil spirit of rebellion. We as a people make things a lot harder than what they appear all because we do not want to be told anything. We

can always learn something about ourselves and those that we become involved with if we would just slow down and take some time out of our busy schedules to listen.

When We Are Not Listening

A. The enemy creeps in
B. Doubts sets in
C. Needs do not get met
D. Attitudes are formed
E. Boredom sets in
F. Love making become a chore
G. Just dwelling takes place
H. We continue to make the same mistakes

These are negative factors that come from the enemy that causes us to struggle. These negatives can destroy any relationship. But battles can be won before they become warfare when we hear our Father and listen to one another in our commitments.

Understanding is also a big part of communication. We have to understand the person we are committed to in our relationships. To truly understand another person that individual must be willing to allow himself to be known in the relationships by being open and honest. It does not take forever to know if we want to make that person our life-long companions for marriage. When we can know something about a person's childhood, past experiences, past relationships, and spend some wholesome quality time with that person, we can have a better understanding of the person we are in a relationship with as long as they are sincere. When we have not dealt with our own experiences of the past, our understanding is bound to be bad because we have not grown.

As we mature spiritually, we began to understand that, in order for us to communicate with one another, we have to maintain the proper attitudes, be able to deal with anger appropriately, and be truthful with one another. We begin to understand that we have to make time for communication in order to listen with an open heart. We learn how to deal with conflicts without judging one another, accusing one another, attacking one another, and always wanting to be right. The right communication causes both individuals to win.

The word of our Father tells us "in all thy wisdom get an understanding". (See Proverbs 4:7, KJV). Spiritual understanding is awesome. It is not to be compared with worldly understanding that is based on what we think or what someone else told us that goes against our Father's word. When we possess spiritual understanding it causes us to know how to really communicate with one another the right way. We begin to understand that we must spend quality time with our Father in order to have healthy relationships with others. Spiritual understanding causes us to understand the person we are committed to in our relationships are a lifetime of learning, and that is better than any movie we could ever see.

Spiritual Understanding causes us to understand what a person is not saying. There are times we are led to communicate and there are times we are led to be silent. In our commitments with our mates, when we are not told verbally that we are loved and it is shown by their actions, we will know their love for us. When we do get feed back from our mates and we begin to see immediate results about what we communicated, we will know we have been heard.

Chapter Five

Dedicated To The One I Love

Beloved, let us love one another; for love is of God,
and everyone that loveth is born of God, and knoweth God.
He that loveth not knoweth not God; for God is Love.
I John 4:7-8, KJV

This chapter is dedicated to the One I Love. The One who loves us all enough to carry us through our struggles when we allow Him. The One that gives us what we need deep inside to hold on to what we cannot see in order to move forward while going through our struggles. The One that equips us with the faith we need to trust Him in spite of whatever struggle we may be facing at the time. The One who helps us to recognize any unseen evil spirit we are going up against while going through our struggles. The only One in the earth who can give us the wisdom to understand Love and what Love is once we genuinely commit to Him.

The Spirit of Love existed back in that perfect beginning before any creation and before the foundation of this earth age. The Spirit of Love existed long before we came into the knowledge of love and could form our own opinions of love and what love meant. We as a people took a perfect spirit and made the Spirit of Love to be what we wanted based on our wants, feelings, needs, desires, and our own opinions. Most of us have an opinion about the Spirit of Love and what love is to each of us.

In our relationships here on earth we express Love in different ways. Although we express love differently; however the characteristics of love never change. There is a love we should have for our children. When children are disciplined, this is an expression of love. It teaches them at a young age that there are consequences for the choices they make that are good and bad in this life here on earth. When children are being prepared to function in this life, this is an expression of Love. This teaches them how to make the right decisions based on the word of our Father. When children are not given everything they lust after, this is an expression of love. This keeps them from growing up believing they can have anything they want and causes them to know some things they ask for are not good for them at the time. When children can be given back to our Father, this is an expression of Love. They learn how to depend on our Father for situations they face in life, as they see us praying and depending on Him.

There is a love we should have for our parents. When we can respect our parents in spite of what we may think, this is an expression of love. It causes us to respect those in authority over us even when we disagree. When we can obey our parents in their homes in spite of what we may want to do, this is an expression of love. This keeps us from growing up thinking we are above rules and regulations. When we can listen to our parents without talking back, this is an expression of love. We are learning early on how to control our tongues and listen. When we can show our parents that we care for them, this is an expression of love. This causes us to honor our parents and spend quality time with our parents.

There is a love we should have for our friends. When we can listen to our friends without judging them, this is an expression of love. This teaches us how to accept others for who they are. When we can keep in confidence what was shared to us by our close friends, this is an expression of love. We learn from this situation that it is a blessing when someone feels close enough to share some of their experiences with us and not to gossip about what was shared. When our friends feel down and we can lift them up, this is an expression of love. This teaches us how to speak life to an individual.

There is a love we should have for each other in our marriages. When intimacy is shared between a man and a woman, this is an expression of love. This causes couples to share with one another, give to one another, and listen to one another. When couples can really communicate with one another, this is an expression of love. This means that they understand one another, they know one another, they are truthful with one another, and they are a blessing to one another. When a man and a woman can submit one to another, this is an expression of love. This causes man to understand what it is like for his wife to submit to him as he submits to word of our Father.

The characteristics of Love did not change in any of these given situations, only the temperaments. The difference is the lovemaking that is shared between a man and a woman in their marriages. This temperament should not be shared with our children, our parents, our relatives, our friends, or our neighbors thus it becomes something other than what love is. There is always an act of the will involved with the characteristics of Love and our feelings are the fruits of those actions. As we live our lives here on earth with no real relationship with our Father, we cannot and will not understand the depths of love and what love is. We cannot know what Love is when we have not accepted the Spirit of God into our hearts. We cannot experience the fullness of Love when there is no real relationship with our Lover.

Some individuals believe that forcing someone to be with them, someone lying to them about a situation just to keep from hurting them, someone saying they are in love with them but making excuses to commit to them, someone trying to control them, or someone that wants to sex them to death before marriage are expressions of love. Some individuals believe love is without discipline, being able to have their way, someone being possessive with them, or being obsessed with them are expressions of love. There are those who believe someone fighting over them, arguing over them, or stalking them are expressions of love. There are individuals that really believe that kind of behavior makes them special.

But when we do not have a relationship with our Father, we will not understand these situations are not called love. This is drama. A lot of us experience this kind of drama in our lives daily because we do not understand the difference. A lot of us love the drama because we are insecure and do not understand who we are in Christ. When we do not have an intimate relationship with our Father, we will believe the sins that are manifested as a result of us living our lives independent of our Father are expressions of love, because we are void of understanding.

Most of what we believe about love has a lot to do with the examples that were set before us, what was shown to us, how we were affected by what was shown, and our experiences in our relationships. This is the extent of what we know about love until we begin to establish a for real relationship with our Father and accept Jesus Christ as our personal Savior. Once we fall in Love with our Father and begin to establish a relationship with Him, we will begin to experience real true genuine love. We may not understand all the characteristics of love along with its many temperaments but we will begin to know what love is not.

When we are in a relationship with someone who wants to control us, the Holy Spirit of God inside of us will raise up against the controlling spirit and warn us that something is wrong with this relationship. The Spirit of God inside of us cannot be controlled by force. The Spirit of God inside of us will not be controlled by force. The Spirit of God does not control us. We are given a free-will to choose whom we will allow to be Lord of our lives. The Spirit of Love causes us to know the spirit of control is not a characteristic of His. In Deuteronomy 6:5 it reads, "And thou shalt love the Lord thy God with all thine heart, and with all thy soul, and with all thy might." This is a command. Love commands us but does not controls us.

When we are in a relationship with someone who is violent with us prior to marriage even just once, the Holy Spirit of God inside of us will raise up and let us know we should get to stepping out of this relationship. The Spirit of

God inside of us will not tolerate being knocked around by the enemy. The Spirit of God inside of us will not tolerate being cursed out and beat down daily by the enemy. If this type of behavior happens prior to marriage, more than likely it will take place in the marriage if the abuser continues to live his life independent of our Father. If we choose to stay in this type of abusive relationship prior to marriage, we are letting the flesh control our actions. We certainly cannot blame our Father if we choose to enter into a marriage with this bad spirit because He allowed us to know what we were dealing with. The Spirit of Love does not beat upon us. We are being shown that for the time being this individual is lost.

When we are in a relationship with someone that has admitted to falling in and out of love with several people and now they claim to be in love with us, the Holy Spirit of God inside of us will raise up and let us know this individual is confused. The Spirit of Love causes us to understand that we do not fall in and out of love. The Spirit of Love causes us to understand that our Father does not fall in and out of love with us. He hates our sins but loves His creation.

When we are in a relationship with someone prior to marriage who does not want to spend any quality time getting to know us, the Holy Spirit of God inside of us will raise up and let us know this individual is not for real. The Spirit of God inside of us causes us to understand that just as we have to spend quality time with our Father to have a relationship with Him, we must spend quality time with each other to establish a relationship with one another. The Spirit of Love causes us to understand when someone does not want to spend quality time getting to know us, or someone does not want us to know them, they do not really care for us. These are selfish individuals. When we really understand who we are in Christ, our tolerance level for the games individuals play becomes unbearable. There are times in our lives when we can be deceived, but it will not take us long to know when someone is not for real.

The Spirit of Love comes from the Spirit of God because God is Love and Love is of God. If we cannot Love God we cannot love others genuinely, and we certainly cannot love ourselves when we do not have the Spirit of Love operating within us. (See I John 4: 7-8, KJV). We cannot have the Spirit of Love operating inside of us if we have not accepted Jesus Christ as our Lord and Savior and all that He is to God our Father. (See I John 4:15&16, KJV).

The Spirit of Love brings with him many characteristics to equip us for whatever struggles we face in life while we are here on earth. There are many different characteristics of good spirits out there in this cosmos just full of Love waiting to take root in our lives, with the characteristics we need to help us in our daily battles with the unseen. These good spirits come into our lives to bring us the strength we need to stand in our struggles, and the wisdom to understand how we should handle our struggles while we are here on earth. They bring into our lives the characteristics of Love that we are lacking at the time, for any struggles that we are faced with. These struggles may be on our jobs, in our marriages, with our families, children, neighbors, friends, among other saints of God, or within each of us. They will not force themselves upon us any more than our Father will force us to love Him. We must be willing to allow these good spirits to come into our lives and take root in our hearts, in order that we may become all that our Father created us to be in this life, for His glory.

Some of the many different characteristics of the Spirit of Love are:

A. The Spirit of Action
B. The Spirit of Choice
C. The Spirit of Commitment
D. The Spirit of Creativity
E. The Spirit of Forgiveness
F. The Spirit of Faith
G. The Spirit of Grace
H. The Spirit of Patience
I. The Spirit of Peace
J. The Spirit of Submission

K. The Spirit of Knowledge
L. The Spirit of Understanding
M. The Spirit of Wisdom
N. The Spirit of Counsel

The Spirit of Love is infinite with its many different characteristics he can bring into our lives. This book could not contain them all, neither can my finite mind. So I am grateful for what I have been allowed to know Amen.

These good spirits are beings created by our Father. (See Psalms 68:17), (Hebrews 12:22), & (Rev 5:11, KJV). These spirits are the Holy Angels of God that stood against satan back in the world that was before the foundation of this earth age. These are the angels that have remained Holy throughout their existence. There is rank and order among these unfallen angels. The Seraphims are considered to be the highest-ranking order of the hierarchy of angels. Isaiah 6 speaks of these angels as "having six wings, two covering the face, two covering the feet, two used for flying." They were described as flying above the throne of God singing His praise. Cherubims are the second highest-ranking order of angels. These angels are the first to be mentioned in the Bible in Genesis 3:24. They were placed by God to guard the gates of Eden. Thrones are the third-ranking order of angels. They were also know as the "Wheels" and the "Many-eyed ones." Ezekiel describes these angels as having "four wings and four faces. (Ezekiel 1:13-19 KJV). Dominions are the fourth-ranking order of Angels. (See Colossians 1:16, KJV). Virtues are the fifth-ranking order of angels. These angels were particular involved with people struggling with their faith. (II Peter 2:5, KJV). They were also called the angels of miracles, encouragement and blessings. The sixth-ranking order of angels are Powers. These angels protect our souls from the evil beings and acts as ministers to our Father who avenge evil in the world. Romans 13:1 states, "Let every Soul be subject unto the higher powers" These angels also protects our souls from the evil demons. The seventh-ranking order of angels are the

Principalities. They are described as the angels who protect religions. Also considered to be the guardians over the nations and leaders of the world. (Colossians 1:16, KJV). The eight ranking order of angels are the Archangels. These angels carry our Father's messages to humans. (See Daniel 10:10-12, KJV). They are ultimately in command of our Father's armies of angels who are constantly in spiritual warfare with the forces of evil and the fallen angels. (See Revelation 12:7, KJV). The ninth-ranking order is called angels. These angels are the closest to humanity. Although some of these angels come into our lives to bring us what we need for our own individual struggles with the unseen, their primary place is at the throne of God. (See Revelation 5:11, KJV). They go about doing the Will of our Father in Heaven and on earth.

Our angels are with us from the time we are born until our lives end here on earth. These good spirits observe us all. They know when we are about to go into our struggles and they see how we handle our struggles. They know when we are coming out of our struggles. They are around to care for our physical safety and our well being as we come out of our struggles. They also protect us from those dangers we do not know about that lurk ahead of us in this life while we are here on earth. They can appear in human form, they spoke as men, took men by the hand, and ate men's food. (See Genesis 18, 19:1-3 KJV). These angels know what characteristics each of us need in our lives for our own individual battles with the unseen. They are present in our lives to help us stand against satan along with his many evil forces while we are here on earth, just as they stood against satan back in the world that was, before the foundation of this earth age. (See Luke 22:43, KJV). We have the same awesome power as the angels when we allow ourselves to be used by the Spirit of Love along with its many characteristics. We need to recognize the power our Father has given us, regardless of what other individuals think or say about our struggles. We truly can do all things, go through any struggle, and accept what our Father allows

without question, when we accept Jesus Christ as our Lord and Savior and all that He is to our Father.

The Spirit of Action is what caused the word of
God to become flesh and dwell among us.
John 1:14, KJV

The Spirit of Action comes into our lives and causes us to know that in this life we have to work. The Spirit of Action causes us to be productive, effective on our jobs, active in our relationships, and work in our marriages. The Spirit of Action motivates us to do what we are capable of doing when we become lazy about doing what we have the capability to do. The Spirit of Action causes us to reach our full potential in life and do the best we can do at whatever task we take.

We can see the Spirit of Action demonstrated by our Father in his word all throughout the scriptures. Our Father preparing a body for himself and coming to this earth in the person of Jesus Christ is an Action by our Father that comes from His Spirit of Love. (See Hebrews 10:5-7, KJV). Our Lord and Savior Jesus Christ willingly coming to this earth to die for our sins knowing all of us were not going to accept Him is an Action by our Lord and Savior Jesus Christ that comes from His Spirit of Love. (See Philippians 2:7-10, KJV). The fact that our Father blesses us in spite of who we are is an Action by our Father that comes from His Spirit of Love. (See Psalms 8:4-6, KJV).

When we allow ourselves to be used by the Spirit of Action, we will pray together in good times and when the enemy is allowed to perfect us. The Spirit of Action causes families to function as a team in their homes and a unit outside their homes. The Spirit of Action causes us to lead by example, to teach by example, and to be the example. The Spirit of Action gives us a readiness to do what God has called us to do. The Spirit of Action moves us to seek Christian Counseling together when we cannot seem to work through conflicts on our own. The Spirit of Action causes us to show love for one another.

When the Spirit of Action has taken root in our hearts, we will study the word of God together as a family in order to know what God requires of us, as opposed to going by what we think, or how it was when we were growing up. The Spirit of Action causes us to make an impact on the lives of others in some capacity. The Spirit of Action causes us to share the knowledge that our Father has allowed us to know for the good of others. The Sprit of Action causes us to reach out and give to those that are less fortunate for all the right reasons. The Spirit of Action causes us to get up off our rumps and do whatever it takes for our commitments to work. The Spirit of Action causes us to get results in the things that we do in this life.

The Spirit of Creativity is what caused all things that are in Heaven and in the earth, visible and invisible, whether they be thrones, dominions, principalities or powers were all created by God and for God. See Colossians 1:16, KJV

The Spirit of Creativity comes into our lives to bring out the best in each of us. The Spirit of Creativity causes us to be shaped into what God called us to be for our specific purposes while here on earth. The Spirit of Creativity causes us to conceive in our minds different ways to please one another in our marriages, and uses us to bring what we conceived to pass when we allow Him.

We can see the Spirit of Creativity demonstrated by our Father in his word all throughout the scriptures. Angels created by God that surround the throne of God to carry out his purposes for us while we are here on earth is Creativity by our Father that comes from His Spirit of Love. (See Psalms 68:17, KJV)

Man that was created in the image and the likeness of our Father is Creativity by our Father that comes from His Spirit of Love. (See Genesis 1:26-27, KJV). The formation of how a sperm and an egg can come together forming human beings of different races with different personalities having a mind, a body, a soul, and a spirit that cannot be explained by man is Creativity by our Father that comes from His Spirit of Love. (See Genesis 3:16, KJV).

When we allow ourselves to be used by the Spirit of Creativity, it gives us the personality to understand that if we courted each other outside our marriages then we should continue to court one another in our marriages. The Spirit of Creativity causes us to understand that if we treated each other good when we were courting, we should continue to treat each other good in our marriages. The Spirit of Creativity causes us to become affectionate to one another in our marriages and causes us to understand that affection is the setting for our marriages and making love is the result of that affection. The Spirit of Creativity causes us to understand that affection is hugging one another, spending quality time with one another, listening to one another, touching one another, giving one another eye contact, respecting one another, blessing one another with good wholesome communication, and trusting one another.

When the Spirit of Creativity has taken root in our hearts, we will understand the marriage bed is flawless, and whatever man and woman do in their marriage that is comfortable for the two of them sexually, our Father smiles down on it. The Spirit of Creativity causes us to nurture one another so we can continue to stay alive in our homes and our marriages will continue to mature and grow spiritually. The Spirit of Creativity keeps boredom from entering into our marriages.

The Spirit of Creativity causes us to become romantic with one another. It also causes us to understand that being romantic is imagining in our minds getting away for the weekend staying right at home just pretending we are in our favorite places. The Spirit of Creativity can cause us to dress up as if we are going out to dinner and have dinner by candle light right at home. The Spirit of Creativity can cause us to pitch a tent and go camping right in our own back yards.

The Spirit of Creativity will cause us to walk and hold hands together without being concerned about the enemy calling us henpecked or whipped because he does not want to see Christian marriages working out. The Spirit of Creativity causes us to have gatherings right at home as if we were in a park. The Spirit of Creativity causes us to know that even our lovemaking in our marriages should be done to the glory of God. The Spirit of Creativity causes us to want to please each other in our marriages.

The Spirit of Choice caused God our Father to Choose us in him before the foundation of this earth age
See Ephesians 1:4, KJV

The Spirit of Choice causes us to be accountable for our actions. The Spirit of Choice causes us to understand that our Father will not force us to love each other, no more than He will force us to love Him. The Spirit of Choice causes us to realize, that going to hell is a decision we choose to make. On the other hand the Spirit of Choice causes us to know if we want to live eternally with our Father we must accept Jesus Christ as our Lord and Savior and all that He is to God our Father. The Spirit of Choice causes us to choose right, to do right, to live right, in the midst of an out of order society.

We can see the Spirit of Choice demonstrated by our Father in his word all throughout the scriptures. Our Father saving those of us that believe in our hearts by faith that Jesus Christ died and was raised from the dead, is a Choice by our Father that comes from His Spirit of Love. (See Romans 9, KJV). Our Father chastising those that are His and those that He loves, just as he instructs us to chastise our children out of love, is a Choice by our Father that comes from His Spirit of Love. (See Hebrews 12:6-7, KJV). Rewarding each of us for the things that we have done in the body in this life is a Choice by our Father that comes from His Spirit of Love. (See Revelation 22:12, KJV).

When we allow ourselves to be used by the Spirit of Choice, we will choose to Love the person we are married to just as our Father has chosen to Love us, in spite of who we are. The Spirit of Choice causes us to refuse to follow satan. The Spirit of Choice causes us to really treat others the way

we want to be treated, and it causes us to do what our Father has instructed us to do even when it hurts us. The Spirit of Choice causes us to know the difference between right and wrong, good and evil.

When the Spirit of Choice has taken root in our hearts, it causes us to give ourselves totally to each other. It also causes us to make decisions to stand for right so we will not fall for everything wrong. The Spirit of Choice causes us to commit to be loyal to one another. The Spirit of Choice causes us understand that there are consequences for the decisions we make. The Spirit of Choice causes us to understand that withholding any part of ourselves in our marriages, is not of God and allows the enemy to creep in.

The Spirit of Commitment causes us to
commit unto the Lord and trust in him
Psalms 37:5, KJV

The Spirit of Commitment causes us to understand that we must first commit to God our Father in order for us to understand how to commit to another person. The Spirit of Commitment gives us staying power in a marriage with true believers. The Spirit of Commitment causes us to tell the enemy he cannot have, he cannot take, and he cannot come between what God has given us. The Spirit of Commitment causes us to have an intimate relationship with our Father.

We see the Spirit of Commitment demonstrated by our Father in his word all throughout the Scriptures. The promise our Father made to us that he will never leave us or forsake us, is a Commitment by our Father that comes from His Spirit of Love. (See Hebrews 13:5, KJV). The promise our Father made to us that he will be with us even when this earth age has ended, is a Commitment by our Father that comes from His Spirit of Love. (See Matthew 28:20, KJV). The rainbow as a sign of the covenant that God made to Noah that the earth nor flesh will not be destroyed by waters of a flood as it was in the days of Noah, is a Commitment by

our Father that comes from His Spirit of Love. (See Genesis 9:11-17, KJV).

When we allow ourselves to be used by the Spirit of Commitment, we will stand and keep on standing when we feel we have done all we can do, and when we do not want to do any more. The Spirit of Commitment causes us to be dedicated to our obligations and causes us to take authority over what our Father has left us to do. The Spirit of Commitment causes us to compliment each other in our marriages.

When the Spirit of Commitment has taken root in our hearts, it causes us to hang together in our marriages even when the spirit of division tells us to walk out, leave, give up, and go file for a divorce. The Spirit of Commitment causes us to protect each other in our marriages. It causes us to not be ashamed of each other in our marriages and to be rooted and grounded in the word of God. The Spirit of Commitment keeps us from being easily turned on to attractive but false doctrine. It causes us to remember the promise and obligation we made to our Father first, second to our marriage, and third to each other.

The Spirit of Grace causes God our Father to offer salvation to a world that deserves judgment but saves all who believe on his son Jesus Christ Ephesians 2:7&8, KJV

The Spirit of Grace causes our Father to give us favor, and it is free. The Spirit of Grace causes things to happen for us that no man can explain. It causes a way to be made out of no way and our Father to come up with ways that never entered our minds as to how a struggle will unfold for us.

We see the Spirit of Grace demonstrated in the word by our Father all throughout the Scriptures. Lot and his daughters spared from the destruction that took place in Sodom and Gomorrah, is an act of Grace by our Father that comes from His Spirit of Love. (See Genesis 19, KJV). David showing kindness to Mephibosheth, the son of

Jonathan, and commanding that he be taken out of Lodebar and given all that pertained to Saul and his house is an act of Grace that comes from the Spirit of Love (See II Samuel 9:6-9, KJV). Our Father giving back to Nebuchadnezzar all that he allowed to be taken from him when he recognized Him as the Most High as he praised, blessed, and honored Him is an act of Grace by our Father that comes from His Spirit of Love. (See Daniel 4:34, KJV).

When we allow ourselves to be used by the Spirit of Grace, it causes us to know we might not get a second chance to do what our Father has instructed us to do. The Spirit of Grace causes us to be thankful for what our Father has allowed us to accomplish. The Spirit of Grace causes us to realize the best God gave us is right at home. The Spirit of Grace causes us to be thankful for each other.

When the Spirit of Grace has taken root in our hearts, it causes us to realize we do not have the time we think we have to get right, to do right, to be right, and live right. The Spirit of Grace causes us to realize every day we get up is a day God has given us to right a wrong. The Spirit of Grace causes us to realize we are all one step away from being jobless, one step away from being homeless, and one step away from death. The Spirit of Grace causes us to be humble by being appreciative of what our Father has allowed each of us to have. It makes us grateful for what our Father has allowed each of us to know. The Spirit of Grace causes us to know we should not take for granted what our Father has given us and it causes us to know that our time here on earth is short compared to our Father's time operating in eternity.

The Spirit of Peace causes the Peace of God,
which passeth all understanding,
to keep our hearts and minds through Christ Jesus.
Philippians 4:7, KJV

The Spirit of Peace causes the spirit of fear to be removed from our hearts and it keeps us in our right minds while going through our struggles. The Spirit of Peace keeps us from getting anxious and it causes us to have inner contentment. The Spirit of Peace makes us stress free and worry free regardless of how difficult our struggles may be.

We can see the Spirit of Peace demonstrated by our Father in His word all throughout the Scripture. Paul praising God for the thorn in his flesh, his weaknesses, his insults, and his persecution, is an action of Peace that comes from the Spirit of Love. (See II Corinthians 12: 8-10, KJV). The reviving of Jacob's spirit to learn that his son Joseph was alive after believing he was dead, is an action of Peace by Jacob that comes from the Spirit of Love. (See Genesis 45:27- 28, KJV). The quietness and rest from all their enemies that Israel had during the reign of King Solomon on earth is an action of Peace from our Father, that comes from the Spirit of Love. (See I Chronicles 22:9, KJV).

When we allow ourselves to be used by the Spirit of Peace, we will step out on faith and not doubt. The Spirit of Peace causes us to know our battles have already been won and we are victorious. The Spirit of Peace causes us to know our time is not the same as our Father's time, but He is always on time for us operating in eternity. The Spirit of Peace causes us to know that the struggles our Father allows us to go through, builds character in us. The Spirit of Peace gives us a calmness and we are taken to an even higher level in Christ Jesus.

When the Spirit of Peace has taken root in our hearts, it causes us to sit back and allow our Father to fight our battles. The Spirit of Peace causes us to understand the end results of our struggles, as opposed to what is happening in our lives at the moment. The Spirit of of Peace causes us to

praise our Father in the midst of our struggles and it keeps us from being afraid when evil is all around us. The Spirit of Peace causes us to know without struggles we would not grow. The Spirit of Peace causes us to have the Spirit of Joy and the Spirit of Happiness.

The Spirit of Forgiveness causes God our Father to
forgive us every time we confess our sins,
he is faithful and just to forgive us of our sins,
and to cleanse us from all unrighteousness.
See I John 1:9, KJV

The Spirit of Forgiveness comes into our lives to keep the spirit of anger and the spirit of hate along with its many hidden disguises from settling into our hearts. The Spirit of Forgiveness causes us to be open hearted. The Spirit of Forgiveness causes us to understand we must forgive one another, in order for God our Father to forgive us. The Spirit of Forgiveness keeps us from sitting in denial.

We see the Spirit of Forgiveness shown by our Father in His word all throughout the Scriptures. Esau having compassion on his brother Jacob for tricking him out of his birthright and stealing his blessings, is an act of Forgiveness that comes from the Sprit of Love. (See Genesis 27:28-36, KJV). The mercy of God towards David that he would not die when he earnestly prayed about killing Ur iah the Hittite and committing adultery with his wife Bathsheba, is an act of Forgiveness by our Father that comes from His Spirit of Love. (See II Samuel 11:17-27, &12:13, KJV).

Joseph loving his brothers in spite of them casting him into a pit and selling him to the Ishmaelites knew as time past, that God meant his struggles for good in order that the purpose of God through Joseph would be carried out, is an act of Forgiveness by Joseph that comes from the Spirit of Love. (See II Samuel 11:17-27, &12:13, KJV).

When we allow ourselves to be used by the Spirit of Forgiveness, we can keep moving forward in spite of our struggles. The Spirit of Forgiveness causes us to pray for those who inflict hurt upon us when they allow themselves to be used by the enemy. The Spirit of of Forgiveness causes us to receive from others "I am sorry", "I was wrong", "I made a mistake", and "forgive me". The Spirit of Forgiveness causes us to sincerely forgive others when they have wronged us.

When the Spirit of Forgiveness has taken root in our hearts, we can love the unlovable and forgive the unforgivable. The Spirit of Forgiveness causes us to deal with our wrongs and leave them in the past. The Spirit of Forgiveness causes us to "kiss and make up." The Spirit of Forgiveness causes us to realize we all make mistakes and that nothing down here on earth is perfect. The Spirit of Forgiveness causes us to admit when we are wrong and it causes us to become Godly sorrowful for what we have done to others and make a conscious effort to do better. The Spirit of Forgiveness keeps us from blaming others for our actions.

The Spirit of Patience causes God our Father to count it all joy when we fall into various trials, knowing this, that the testing of our faith worketh patience. James 1:2&3,KJV.

The Spirit of Patience causes us to understand we are in a spiritual warfare. The Spirit of Patience brings into our lives endurance to deal with our struggles. The Spirit of Patience gives us self-control to allow our Father to fight our battles. The Spirit of Patience gives us long-suffering to bare our struggles. The Spirit of Patience keeps us from complaining. The Spirit of Patience equips us to wait on our Father until His Will is clear to us in our lives. The Spirit of Patience causes us to know our Father does not lie and that He will do what He promises.

We can see the Spirit of Patience shown by our Father in His word all throughout the Scripture. Our Father waiting in the days of Noah as he preached to unsaved people while preparing the ark, is an act of Patience by our Father that comes from His Spirit of Love. (I Peter 3:17, KJV). Job enduring his suffering and remaining faithful to God is an

act of Patience that comes from the Spirit of Love. (See Job 1-37, KJV).

Jacob agreeing to serve Laban for seven years to have his younger daughter Rachel for his wife is an act of Patience by Jacob that comes from the Spirit of Love. (See Genesis 29:18-20, KJV).

When we allow ourselves to be used by the Spirit of Patience, it causes us to understand we are all at different levels in our spiritual growth. The Spirit of Patience causes us to know what affects one of us, affects the other in our commitments. The Spirit of Patience causes us to hang in our struggles until our Father says we can move on. The Spirit of Patience causes us to know we cannot rush our Father for nothing that we want in this life. The Spirit of Patience causes us to understand time brings about a change in ourselves and and in others.

When the Spirit of Patience has taken root in our hearts, it causes us to wait on our Father. The Spirit of Patience causes us to become spiritually mature. The Spirit of Patience causes our Faith to be increased. The Spirit of Patience causes us to know for ourselves just how dedicated we are to commitments. The Spirit of Patience causes us to understand everything happens for a reason and our Father knows what is best for us.

The Spirit of Submission causes the devil to flee from us when we submit to God.
James 4:7, KJV

The Spirit of Submission causes the evil spirit of pride to be removed from our hearts. The Spirit of Submission causes the heads of households to understand they are under the authority of the word and over authority in their homes. The Spirit of Submission causes each of us to understand we are all accountable to someone. The Spirit of Submission causes us to surrender our will to the Will of our Father when we want to have our own way. The Spirit of

Submission causes us to respect those that are in authority over us as unto the Lord and it causes us to obey God's word.

We see the Spirit of Submission shown by our Father in His word all throughout the Scriptures. The Holy Angels of God submitting to the word of God and the word of God submitting to our Father, is an action of Submission by the Godhead that comes from His Spirit of Love. (See Genesis 1:27, KJV). Hosea's obedience to our Father to love, to submit, and to honor, his wife in spite of her unfaithfulness is an action of Submission that comes from the Spirit of Love. (See Hosea 1:2-3, KJV). Moses's obedience to our Father each time he was told to go before Pharoah to tell him to set the children of Israel free, is an action of Submission that comes from the Spirit of Love. (See Exodus 3, KJV).

When we allow ourselves to be used by the Spirit of Submission, it causes us to step up and take our roles that our Father has given us. The Spirit of Submission causes us to listen to each other, as opposed to listening to what someone else thinks about what is best for us in our commitments. The Spirit of Submission causes us to want God's Will to be done in our lives.

When the Spirit of Submission has taken root in our hearts, it causes us to have an intimate relationship with our Father. The Spirit of Submission causes us to have an intimate relationship with each other. The Spirit of Submission causes us to submit one to another. The Spirit of causes us to commit to each other. The Spirit of Submission keeps us from outright rebelling against the word of our Father.

The Spirit of Faith is the substance of things hoped for and the evidence of things not seen. Hebrews 1:1,KJV

This Spirit of Faith causes us to believe our Father can work out every struggle we face. The Spirit of Faith causes us to step out on trust and believe our Father will supply our every need. The Spirit of Faith causes us to know our Father protects us from what we do not see.

We can see the Spirit of Faith shown by our Father in the word all throughout the Scriptures. Abraham going to a place without knowing where or why he was going and trusting God to protect him along the way, is an act of Faith that comes from the Spirit of Love. (Hebrews 11:9&10, KJV). David taking his eyes off what he saw when he went up against Goliath the giant and trusting God to fight this battle through him, is an act of Faith that comes from the Spirit of Love (I Samuel 17: 49-51, KJV). Shadrach, Meshach, and Abednego thrown into the burning fiery furnace for not worshipping the golden image Nebuchadnezzar the King had set up and believing that our Father was able to protect them, is an act of faith that comes from the Spirit of Love. (Daniel 3:17-25, KJV).

When we allow ourselves to be used by the Spirit of Faith, we are confident our Father hears and answers our prayers, according to His Will for our lives. The Spirit of Faith causes us to know our Father is obligated to do what he promises us He will do according to His Word, and He has never turned His back on His Word with the exception of dying on the cross for mankind. The Spirit of Faith causes us to know our prayers are protected. The Spirit of Faith causes us to know our Father carries us through our struggles. The Spirit of Faith causes us to hold on to what we cannot see. The Spirit of Faith causes us to know we deal with the possible and our Father deals for us with the impossible.

When the Spirit of Faith has taken root in our hearts, we can stand on the word of God and go forth boldly, knowing our Father goes before us fighting our battles. The Spirit of Faith causes us to sit back and watch our Father show up and show out in our lives, fighting our battles and shaming the enemy. The Spirit of Faith causes us to trust our Father for what we do not understand. The Spirit of Faith causes us to take our Father at His word and it causes us to accept what our Father allows. The Spirit of Faith causes us to know without a doubt our Father is still directing the affairs of men down here on earth. The Spirit of Faith causes us to know the enemy cannot take away anything our Father has given us. The Spirit of Faith causes us to trust the word of our Father regardless of what man has said or believes. The Spirit of Faith causes us to know our Father cannot lie. The Spirit of Faith causes us to know everything our Father has said in His word will come to pass in this life here on earth and in the life to come.

"And the Spirit of the Lord shall rest upon him, the Spirit of Wisdom and Understanding, the Spirit of Counsel and Might, the Spirit of Knowledge and the fear of the Lord, And shall make him of quick understanding in the fear of the Lord; and he shall not judge after the sight of his eyes, neither reprove after the hearing of his ears" Isaiah 11:2&3, KJV

The Spirit of Wisdom causes us to understand life and how it really is for the saints of God while we are here on earth. The Spirit of Understanding causes us to know we are in this world but not of this world. The Spirit of Counsel instructs us to seek our Father for every struggle we face. The Spirit of Might gives us the strength to deal with any struggles our Father allows when it is not a struggle we have brought on ourselves.

We can see the Spirit of Wisdom, the Spirit of Knowledge, the Spirit of Understanding, the Spirit of Might, and the Spirit of Counsel shown by our Father in His word all throughout the Scriptures. The insight that was given to Solomon as a child to be able to judge the people of God during his reign as king on earth, is an action of Wisdom and Understanding by Solomon that comes from the Spirit of Love. (See I Kings 3:12, KJV).

The secret things of God being revealed to Daniel in order that he would know, understand and interpret dreams is an action of Knowledge, Wisdom, and Understanding that comes from the Spirit of Love. (See Daniel 1:14, KJV).

Ezekiel being called out by God to go forth and prophesy to the house of Israel as God spoke through Ezekiel each time He wanted to get a message over to His people, is an action of Counsel given to Ezekiel by our Father, that comes from His Spirit of Love. (See Ezekiel 3:26-27, KJV).

Abigal, the wife of Nabal, sent by God to meet David and his men with blessings and advice in order that the household of Nabal would be spared, is an action of Understanding that comes from the Spirit of Love. (See I Samuel 25:18-25, KJV)

Jermiah being called, ordained, and inspired by God before he was formed in his mothers womb, is an action of Counsel by our Father that comes from the Spirit of Love. (See Jeremiah 1:5, KJV).

The Apostle John on the Isle of Patmos giving spiritual eyes to see things past, things present, things to come in the future, and writing down what he saw and heard in order that we may know what is going to take place, is an action of Counsel and Knowledge that comes from the Spirit of Love. (See Revelations).

The strength and force of the armies of King David during his reign on earth are actions of Might that come from the Spirit of Love. (See II Samuel 23:8-39, KJV).

The calling of Isaiah by God to know things that were discussed back in the Counsel of God and foretell what was going to take place in the future is Knowledge that was given to Isaiah by our Father, that comes from His Spirit of Love. (See Isaiah, KJV).

When we allow ourselves to be used by the Spirit of Wisdom, the Spirit of Understanding, the Spirit of Knowledge, the Spirit of Counsel, and the Spirit of Might, we can step outside of self and understand the big picture, battling with the unseen. The Spirit of Understanding causes us to know our struggles are not against each other. The Spirit of Knowledge causes us to understand that we are fighting against the spirit that we are allowing ourselves to be used by. The Spirit of Might gives us the strength to deal with each other when we are allowing ourselves to used by these evil forces satan sends our way.

When the Spirit of Wisdom, the Spirit of Understanding, the Spirit of Knowledge, the Spirit of Counsel and the Spirit of Might have taken root in our hearts, we can recognize the enemies as they come. These good spirits cause us to know what type of evil spirits we are going up against. The Spirit of Wisdom causes our motives to be genuine in the things we do while we are here on earth. The Spirit of Understanding causes us to look at ourselves first, as opposed to expecting someone else to do the right thing when we know deep within ourselves we are not right. The Spirit of Knowledge causes us to be mindful of why we do the things that we do, say the things we say, and act the way we act. The Spirit of Might causes us to be strong so we will not allow ourselves to be used by the enemies to the point of destruction. The Spirit of Wisdom causes us to understand that in order to receive the blessings of our Father, we must go through some struggles to be able to handle the good things our Father has for us. The Spirit of Understanding causes us to know we have power inside of us that is greater than any evil spirit the enemy sends our way. The Spirit of Knowledge causes us to understand we are no match for the enemy with our strength from the flesh. The Spirit of Counsel directs us in the right way while going through our struggles. The Spirit of Wisdom causes us to learn from our struggles. The Spirit of Understanding keeps us from making the same mistakes over and over again. The Spirit of Knowledge causes us to understand better in order that we may do better. The Spirit of Counsel shows us what we need to see while going through our struggles. The Spirit of Might gives us the strength to supernaturally do what is humanly impossible while going through our struggles. The Spirit of Wisdom causes us to know we cannot play around with the enemy. The Spirit of of Understanding causes us to know satan along with his many evil forces will kill us when we try and go up against them with flesh weapons. The Spirit of Knowledge causes us to remember to speak the word of God to the enemy and for a short time he will back up and leave us alone because there is power in the word of our Father.

The Spirit of Love shows each of us that's professing to be Christians and Saved just how much we love our Father. As we live our life here on earth the Spirit of Love shows each of us that's professing to be Christians and Saved how to do those things our Father has instructed us to do. Above all, the Spirit of Love is a commitment. We are all allowed to know for ourselves how committed we are to our commitments while going through our struggles. We are all allowed to know for ourselves just how dedicated we are to the One we say we are in Love with, when we are in our struggles battling with the unseen.

In our relationships here on earth, our Father instructs us in His word as to how we should live in this life with Him as our example. He has never instructed any of us to do something that He has not already experienced. He has never instructed any of us to do something that He has not already gone through. Because He knows us better than we know ourselves, He knows what we are capable of handling. Everything that is happening now as we live out our lives here on earth has already taken place in another time, before the foundation of this earth age.

Our Father always sets the precedent. He knew before the foundation of this earth age long before it was written and before we came into existence, that He was going to prepare a body for Himself and be born. He knew satan had already polluted this earth with his filthiness. He knew satan was mad because he could not have his way up in Heaven. Satan was angry because he was kicked from Heaven. Our Father knew that satan was just waiting on each of His to be born so satan could try to stop God's plan for our lives. Our Father made a decision to come down to this earth in the person of Jesus Christ to show us by His example. He wanted us all to know that we could live down here on earth in its present condition even with it being jacked up, out of order, polluted by satan, and still carry out our purposes on earth as long as we trusted in Him. He came down to his earth to be our example in order that His people would be little examples of Him to a world system that is lost.

Our Father experienced the same struggles when He walked the earth that we experience now in this life while we are here on earth. He was tested by satan time and time again just as we are in our day and time. He was tried by those that were of satan just as we are in our day and time. He was talked about because of what He stood for just as we are today when we are trying our best to live Holy because we serve a HOLY HOLY HOLY Father. He was accused of things He did not do just as we are accused wrongfully in our day and time because of who we are. He was scorned just as we are in our day and time because of ignorance. He became angry because of sin just as we should be when we see our fellow brothers and sisters in Christ going down the wrong crowded path and it seems as if they do not care. He experienced hurt and pain just as we do in this life while here on earth when we are in our struggles. He wept just as we do when we are grieving the loss of a loved one. He cried just as we do when sin has separated us from our loved ones. Because our flesh is sinful and desires the things of this world, satan thought he could tempt his Creator when He was manifested in the flesh. Satan thought he had it going on just that strong to come up against his Creator, just as some of us down here on earth think we got it going on when we allow ourselves to be used by the many evil forces of satan.

Although He is perfect and we as human beings are not perfect, He has equipped us with all that we need in this life while here on earth, with the Spirit of Love along with its many characteristics. All we have to do is allow them to take root in our lives. When we are allowing the Spirit of Love along with its many characteristics to take root in our lives, this does not mean we will be perfect. We are being perfected in areas of our lives where we are weak. We will find ourselves becoming shaped into what our Father created us to be for our specific purposes while here on earth. We will find ourselves becoming shaped into the image He has for each of us in order that we may be able to serve in the Kingdom Age to come.

Because we are not perfect we are allowed to make mistakes as long as we can learn from our mistakes. We will make mistakes simply because our flesh is sinful; however we should not use our imperfections as an excuse to deliberately make the same type of mistakes time and time again when we know better. There are times in our lives when we are going to allow satan along with his many evil forces to occupy our bodies, but the Holy Spirit of God inside us will let us know right away what we are doing. If a change does not come about in us when we are being convicted we should ask ourselves "am I a child of God or did I belong to satan in the world that was?" Just as our Father knew the spirit of Esau before he was conceived in his mother's womb, He knows our spirits as well. (See Malachi 1:3, KJV). He is the One that places our spirits that is with Him into the bodies of our parents. Our Father knew we did not have a savior back in the world that was, and He knew we could not save ourselves. The Spirit of Love caused our Father to give us all a second chance to be born into this earth age with a free-will to choose for ourselves how we want to spend eternity. We are without an excuse now because we carry Him around inside of us every where we go.

When we allow the many characteristics of the Spirit of Love to take root in our lives, we will not bring a struggle on someone else neither will we allow the enemy to occupy our bodies willingly, by being selfish. The Spirit of Love along with its many characteristics, knows each of us need different temperaments at different times in our lives, depending on what type of struggle we are face with and where we are spiritually.

My brothers and sisters in Christ, we all need to wake and realize the reason there are so many divorces among the Saints of God down here on earth, is because we are not allowing the Spirit of Love along with its many characteristics to take root in our lives. Going to the church building, singing in the choir, studying the word of God, sitting on the deacon bench, ushering, evangelizing, and hearing the word of God means nothing if we do not have an intimate relationship with our Father, and applying what our Father have allowed us to know to our daily lives. All we really have is knowledge of Him according to what we hear from others and read. But can we honestly say we really know Him when we do what we believe is right in our own eyes, without an intimate relationship with Him? The only part of us that we have given Him is our minds when He wants our hearts. When our Father does not have our hearts do we actually believe He accepts us as one of His children? Are we banking on spending eternity with our Father and disregarding our Lord and Savior Jesus Christ? If so, we are in for a rude awakening. There will come a day and a time when all of us on the face of this earth will have to stand before our Father and give an account of the things we have done while here on earth. It is going to be horrible, sad, and shameful when we stand before our Father and He tells some of us to "step aside I don't know you," all because we did what we thought or wanted, as opposed to taking Him at his word. This is why so many of us that professes to be Christians and Saved can know what He has instructed us to do and still continue to live our lives as out-laws outside the kingdom making excuses. We either don't know the Father for ourselves or don't believe the instructions He has left here for us are real.

Our relationships in our marriages have everything to do with our relationship with our Father. When we walk away from each other in our marriages, in reality, we are turning our backs on our Father. When we are rebelling against each other in our marriages, in reality, we are not hearing our Father. When we are not submitting to one another in our marriages, in reality, we are not under subjection to the Word. When we cannot love each other in our marriages, in reality, Love is not in our hearts. We did not give ourselves the responsibilities that we have. They were given before we came on the scene.

Marriage between a man and a woman should be spiritual although not all individuals who come together in a marriage are spiritually minded. Marriage between a man and a woman is deep, although not all individuals who come together in marriage understands the depths of how a marriage should mirror God's image. When a man and a woman go before God and make a covenant, both individuals have to allow the Spirit of Love to take root in their hearts, in order for their marriage to survive. When one person is allowing the Spirit of Love to take root in their heart, and the other person is not allowing the Spirit of Love to take root in their heart, we now have two spirits that disagree. As a result, what we have is a marriage between good spirits and bad spirits which causes us to struggle. It becomes a battle with the unseen. Amos 3:3, KJV tells us that, "two cannot walk together except they be in agreement." In marriages among true believers we should be on one accord in the spirit. We should be allowing the many characteristics of the Spirit of Love to take root in our lives, and desiring Gods' Will for our lives. Two Spirits of God joined together will not disagree to the point where their marriage ends in divorce unless the forces of satan are somewhere in the midst.

When marriages end in divorce, this does not mean that the word of God has changed concerning divorces, nor does this means the word of God contradicts itself concerning divorces. It simply means we did not do the things we were instructed by our Father to do, neither did we allow the Spirit of Love to take root in our hearts, and as a result, a divorce came about. Our Father not only hates divorces but he also hates the way we allow ourselves to be used by satan along with his many evil forces. The Spirit of Love causes each of us to know in our marriages when the forces of satan is lurking around our homes. If Christians marriages are supposed to mirror God's image, God did not intend for His people to live together in their marriages as enemies killing each other slowly. We are called out to be the example in all that we do including in our marriages, so that non believers will know there is a difference in the God we serve, and the gods they serve.

When we are allowing the Spirit of Love along with its many characteristics to take root in our lives, our Father is working out for us our marital struggles. Letting go of our marital struggles does not mean for us to separate ourselves from our marriages, run to the divorce court, or stop doing what our Father has instructed us to do. It is time for us to examine ourselves. To stop pointing the blame and recognize whom we are allowing ourselves to be used by. Are we professing to have given our lives to Christ and continued to live like out-laws, trying to hold on to the past because an evil force will allow us to? Are we looking for changes in our mates before we make some changes in ourselves? Are we abusing the power our Father has given us and using the Spirit of Submission as an excuse for others to go along with our wrongs? Do we actually believe when we beat the doors of the Church building opening up, this means we are Christians when we are living like out-laws in our homes? Are we allowing the Spirit of Love along with his many characteristics to take root in our lives, or satan along with his many evil forces to occupy our bodies?

Because so many marriage among those that profess to be Christians and Saved by our Father are ending in divorce we now tell ourselves and others that "everybody that is together God did not put together." Who can really say whom our Father put together or did not put together besides the two people in a marriage together. These individuals know their own motives for choosing each other in marriage. A marital struggle does not necessarily mean our Father did not put two individuals together. Our Father allows us to go through struggles out of Love for our good. When there are no marital struggles between two individuals in their marriage this does not necessarily mean our Father put these individuals together. When a divorce takes place among those professing to be Christians and Saved this does not necessarily mean our Father did not put these individuals together. He will not make us do what He has instructed us to do and the enemy is happy when another Christian home is torn apart. Each of us know the real reasons behind the things we do even if we never admit it others. At some point in our lives we need to get real and become honest with ourselves. Some of us need to admit to ourselves our marriages did not work out because we were not committed to our Father, we did not understand how to commit, we did not want to be committed, we did not understand our relationships, we thought we wanted to be with someone else, we did not want the responsibility of being married once we got married, we did not want to work in our marriages, we lied about ourselves to get what we wanted, we were in lust, we abused the person we had, and we did not know how to love because we had not accepted love into our hearts. These situations can cause our marriages to end because we are not stepping up and taking on the roles that our Father has given us, not realizing we are being used by the enemy. Most of the time those that are screaming the loudest that God did not put them together with their mates are the ones that have done most of the damage. They know deep within their motives were not good and they were just looking for an excuse to be gone, not realizing they are being tricked by the enemy. Some individuals take so much abuse from the enemy prior to marriage and when marriage to the enemy takes place, they do not want to deal with anything.

Our Father knows the real reasons we have chosen the individuals we are married to. He knows those of us that are standing in our marriages and genuinely committed to him. These individuals can accept what our Father allows without losing their minds. There are times our Father will allow separations to take place among individuals. Remember our Father will not force us to do anything. A separation does not necessarily mean a divorce will take place. Some sometimes we cannot see ourselves until we are by ourselves and some individuals still don't wake up.

Our Father allows each of us to really know how sincere we are ourselves. Can we still love Him in our separation from our spouses? Will we blame our spouses for the things we did with other individuals during our separation? Will we take time to examine ourselves and recognize what drove us to the point of separation? Will we trust our Father to work out for us our marital struggles? Can we continue to say no to the enemy trusting our Father for what we do not understand during our separation? Can we take our eyes and our hears off our spouses during our separation, and continue to be committed to our Father?

Our Father also knows those of us who are using Him as an excuse to stay in an unhealthy marriage and not really trusting him. These individuals try to force their marriage to work because they are afraid of what our Father will allow not realizing they are being used by the enemy. Our Father knows who these individuals are. Some of these individuals will take all kind of abuse just to have a man in their life and our Father knows this. Some of these individuals fear starting over and some do not want to start over. Some of these individuals seem to be more concerned about what other individuals will think and they stay in unhealthy marriages. They walk around trying to convince themselves and others they are doing what they are doing "as unto the Lord". I am not saying individuals should walk away from their marriage. I believe if someone is in a marriage that they really feel is abusive and they decide to stay for all the wrong reasons, they will deal with a lot of unnecessary struggles they are bringing on themselves. If an individual who is abusive leaves and files for a divorce, we should see this action as our Father delivering us from a bad situation. We should praise him because we no longer have that terrible spirit in our homes. When we cannot trust our Father because of what He may allow to happen, we are just using Him as an excuse to stay in unhealthy situations. When we allow the Spirit of Love to take root in our lives, this keeps us from experiencing a lot of headaches and heartaches as we allow our Father to fight our battles. What our Father allows may not be what we want, but He knows what is best for us. He also knows who is suited for each of us. We should choose to put all our confidence in Him because the end results are going to be the Will of God for our lives.

The Spirit of Love along with its many characteristics causes us to wake up and realize we cannot make someone love us, nor can we force someone to love us. Trying to force someone to love us is unnatural and does not come from our

Father. This type of force comes from satan along with his many evil forces and is called "losing one's self." Falling in Love and falling out of Love are not characteristics of the Spirit of Love. This type of force comes from satan along with his many evil forces and is called "lust." Disrespecting each other in our marriages just because we feel as if we can are not characteristics of the Spirit of Love. This type of force comes from satan along with his many evil forces and is called "stupidity."

The Spirit of Love along with its many characteristics causes us to come to grips with the fact that the word of God does not change just because we want to have our way. He causes causes us to come to grips with the fact that our Father means what He has said regardless of who we think we are. He causes us to come to grips with the fact that we may be able to fool individuals some of the time, but we cannot fool our Father at anytime. He causes us to come to grips with the fact that things will not get any better for us while here on earth, until we live better for our Father. He causes us to come to grips with the fact that we cannot walk off into the sunset unrighteously and believe good with follow us. There are times in our lives we have to be put to the same test to know what our Father wants us to know, to understand what our Father wants us to understand, in order that we may become what He desires us to become for our specific purposes.

When the Spirit of Love along with its many characteristics has taken root in our lives it causes the Saints of God to wake up and realize if we are just passing through this life, we must allow their temperaments to shape us up in order for us to be prepared to serve in this life while here on earth, and in the Kingdom of God. The Spirit of Love causes us to treat each other the way we want to be treated. The Spirit of Love causes us to know that Love goes beyond what we can see. The Spirit of Love causes us to know that Love goes beyond what we can feel. The Spirit of Love causes us to know that Love goes beyound what we can touch. The Spirit of Love causes us to keep out-laws and in-laws out of

our marriages and concentrate on what our Father has instructed us to do. The Spirit of Love causes us to accept each other without trying to change each other. The Spirit of Love causes us to know we are special in Christ Jesus and we do not have to take from the forces of satan all of his mess that he tries to inflict upon us. The Spirit of Love causes us to want better so we can allow our Father's Will to be done in our lives, as opposed to thinking we cannot do any better than what we are doing. The devil is a lie. The Spirit of Love keeps us from bringing past mistakes, past relationships, past pains, past hurts, past conflicts into our relationships and inflicting them upon out love ones. The Spirit of Love causes us to know that we must constantly allow its characteristics to take root in our lives on a daily basis. The forces of satan are persistent with trying to snatch up those of us genuinely trying to live for Christ Jesus in this life while here on earth.

When we allow the temperaments from the Spirit of Love along with its many characteristics to take root in our lives, our marriages will survive. Our marriages will be all that our Father intended our marriages to be. Our temperaments keep us from giving the enemy our blessings that our Father has given each of us. Our temperaments causes satan along with his many evil forces to know we are armed and extremely dangerous when we are allowing the Spirit of Love along with its many characteristics to take root in our lives. Our temperaments causes us to come up out our struggles stronger and equipped for our next battle.

When we can stand in our struggles genuinely trusting our Father we come up out of our struggles being what our Father wants us to be *HOLY*, knowing that our purpose is *TO SERVE HIM*, seeing what he wants us to see *OURSELVES FOR WHO WE ARE*, acting the way he wants us to act *SEPARATE AND SET APART*, understanding what he wants us to understand *OUR PURPOSE IN LIFE*, and knowing if we truly love him by *OUR OBEDIENCE TO HIM*.

About The Author

S. LOUISIANA DOBY began her first work of non-fiction in 1996 and completed her debut novel in 1998 titled ***That Which Is Hidden***. A passion to share what our Father has allowed her to know and experience is what inspired this Louisiana native to write. She states that "if she can help one somebody through her writing and that one somebody can help somebody else she will have made an impact on someone's life." After reading ***That Which Is Hidden***, hopefully more Christians will want to stand in their struggles in order to know their specific purpose while here on earth.

This Louisiana native holds a Masters Degree in Christian Counseling Psychology from Christian Bible College and Seminary and is a licensed Christian therapist. She resides in the Arlington, TX area where she works full-time as a professional for a major telecommunications company. Studying the word of God and ministering to others are apart of her daily life. During the evenings and on weekends, she loves exercising, getting together with family and friends, reading, traveling, and writing. She is member of Mount Olive Baptist Church in Arlington, TX and sings in the choir, a member of Black Professionals in Communications, and Black Executive Exchange Program.

www.ingramcontent.com/pod-product-compliance
Ingram Content Group UK Ltd.
Pitfield, Milton Keynes, MK11 3LW, UK
UKHW040016200726
13854UKWH00001B/226